VENGEANCE OF THE LAST ROMAN LEGION

BOOK I

OUT OF THE DARKNESS

MARK CARLSON

MILFORD HOUSE

an imprint of Sunbury Press, Inc.
Mechanicsburg, PA USA

MILFORD HOUSE

an imprint of Sunbury Press, Inc.
Mechanicsburg, PA USA

For information about special discounts for bulk purchases, please contact Sunbury Press Orders Dept. at (855) 338-8359 or orders@sunburypress.com.

To request one of our authors for speaking engagements or book signings, please contact Sunbury Press Publicity Dept. at publicity@sunburypress.com.

FIRST MILFORD HOUSE PRESS EDITION: April 2022

Set in Adobe Garamond Pro | Interior design by Crystal Devine | Cover by Alessandra Smith | Edited by Sarah Peachey.

Publisher's Cataloging-in-Publication Data
Names: Carlson, Mark, author.
Title: Vengeance of the Last Roman Legion: Book I - Out of the Darkness / Mark Carlson.
Description: First trade paperback edition. | Mechanicsburg, PA : Milford House Press, 2022.
Summary: Deep in a French cellar A Roman legion awakens from a self-imposed hibernation. The day has at last come to emerge and wreak revenge on their hated Germanic enemy for a savage massacre. But two thousand years have passed. The world has changed. But their vengeance will not die. A NATO investigator learns of this but cannot believe his evidence. It is true. The Romans are coming. And time is running out for them and their prey.
Identifiers: ISBN : 978-1-62006-642-3 (softcover).
Subjects: FICTION / Thrillers / Suspense | FICTION / Thrillers / Terrorism | FICTION / Alternative History | FICTION / Science Fiction / Military.

Product of the United States of America
0 1 1 2 3 5 8 13 21 34 55

Continue the Enlightenment!

This work is dedicated to my late wife, Jane Marie Carlson (1956–2020), who for twenty-five years was my love, my friend and soul mate. She saw the eagle in me long before I did. She supported my wish to be a writer even when it showed little promise of success. I lost Jane in April of 2020 when I was entering the last phase of editing. For months I was certain I could never write again. But she had sacrificed too much for me to give up and so I sat down to continue the work you are about to read. The eagle has flown. Rest in eternal peace, my beloved.

And to my Lord and Savior, my God and Father. He saved me when my heart was breaking and showed me the way to peace and happiness. I am forever humbled by His love and guidance. To Him I dedicate my life as a Christian and vow to use His gifts to reach others with His word.

CONTENTS

TO THE READER

There are four books in this series. Books I, III, and IV occur in the second decade of the twenty-first century, while Book II goes back to the first century AD. With any fiction work, there has to be an element of reality. Fiction has to be believable. A novel with an impossible plot must be built on a foundation of credibility. In this work, many places, organizations, and technology are real and even familiar to the twenty-first-century reader. The structure and history of the Roman Empire are based on history, as is that of France, Belgium, and Germany. While I freely admit that the story is from my imagination, I would not discount the chance that it *could* come true.

As Thomas Hardy said, "While much is too strange to be believed, nothing is too strange to have actually happened."

The geography and flora of northeastern France, Belgium, and central Germany play a role in this story. Descriptions have been changed to further the credibility of the unfolding drama. While the general terrain, rivers, and mountain ranges exist, the forests and rural areas have been moved or altered to suit the story.

I apologize to the reader for any misunderstanding. For readers familiar with the history of the Roman Army, you may notice that the legion in the story is numbered LIV, for fifty-four. I realize there was never a fifty-fourth legion. So read on, and enjoy. Remember, this is a work of fiction.

Mark Carlson
San Diego, California Summer 2021

LEGION ORGANIZATION

This book contains several instances where certain specific unit names and ranks are mentioned. In order to avoid confusion, below is a breakdown of how a Roman Legion was organized.

1 Legion: 4,800 men each of

10 Cohorts: 480 men each of

6 Centuries: 80 men each of

10 Contubernium: (tent/mess) 8 men each

COHORTS

Cohort I: Primus

Cohort II: Secundus

Cohort III: Tertius

Cohort IV: Quartus

Cohort V: Quintus

Cohort VI: Sextus

Cohort VII: Septimus

Cohort VIII: Octavus

Cohort IX: Nomus

Cohort X: Decimus

CENTURIES

Each cohort has six centuria in three groups of two.

First Century: Pilus Prior

Second Century: Pilus Posterior

Third Century: Princeps Prior

Fourth Century: Princeps Posterior

Fifth Century: Hastatus Prior

Sixth Century: Hastatus Posterior

LEGIO LIV COMMAND STRUCTURE

Legion Commander—Legatus: Lucius Cassius Aquilius

Second in Command—Laticlavius: Marcus Titus

Cohort Commanders—

    Primus Ordanes, Cohort Mars: Septimus Scipio Deo

    Primus Ordanes, Cohort Jupiter: Marius Vitellus

    Primus Ordanes, Cohort Apollo: Clavius Atticus

Century Commander—Centurio

Century Second in Command—Optio

Sergeant—Tessairius

Una Salus Victis Nullam Sperare Salutem

"The one hope of the doomed is not to hope for safety."
—*The Aeneid,* Virgil

"Live not for battles won, but for battles lost."
—Unknown

PROLOGUE

NORTHEASTERN FRANCE, PRESENT DAY

André Robert drove the small tractor carefully down the narrow dirt lane between long rows of tall wooden racks supporting lush, green-leafed grapevines. The sky over his vineyard northeast of Reims, France, was a deep clear blue. The July sun gilded the small fruit like clusters of glowing yellow pearls.

Stout with strong hands, the fifty-five-year-old vintner had skin deeply tanned from a lifetime of working in the sun. His blue eyes glinted like pale sapphires under a weathered wide-brimmed straw hat and a strong brow. As the autumn harvest had approached, he daily spent hours walking the rows and sampling grapes by squeezing tiny amounts of liquid gold onto his tongue to judge when it was time to begin picking.

This morning, he was going to clear a new area for an expansion of the chardonnay. After fitting a bulldozer blade to the rear of the used but lovingly maintained 1995 Deutz-Fahr Agrotron K120, he twisted the ignition key. The diesel engine purred like a big tiger. Driving out of the open-sided equipment shed at the edge of the vineyard, he maneuvered the tractor up the winding dirt track toward the west. Fifteen minutes later, he stopped the machine and stepped down onto the dry soil. Ahead of him, the vineyard sloped gently toward a small stream in a shallow ravine. The air was as crisp as fresh lettuce as he inhaled the sweet scent of his chardonnay grapes. Chardonnay had been his late wife Marie's favorite, and the tang of the ripening grapes never failed to remind him of her. Robert paused for a moment and remembered her soft skin, angelic face, and delicate voice. Marie had enjoyed reading classical literature while sitting on a bench beside the stream.

He climbed back onto the idling tractor and turned onto a rutted trail until he reached a wide field of scrub brush and small evergreens. The land had lain fallow for over twenty years. It had rejuvenated itself from the previous fifty years of cultivation by his father and grandfather.

He drew a faded bandanna from his flannel work shirt pocket. After tying it over his lower face, he pulled on a well-worn pair of leather work gloves. He needed room to maneuver, so he chose a small clearing forty meters off the lane as his starting point. Gunning the 120-horsepower engine, he lowered the gleaming blade and put the tractor into reverse gear. With little effort, Robert made room to move around. With skilled handling of the steering wheel, he cleared out more space, gathering all the brush and soil into a neat pile by the lane. A thin veil of diesel fumes mingled with the dust stirred up by the bulldozer blade. The rumble of the engine battered Robert's ears.

The dust made his eyes tear up, and he paused to wipe them with an ungloved hand. Then he sneezed, once, twice, three times. "Damn this dust," he growled in a weak voice. But Robert knew better. He'd been sneezing and sniffling all morning. Another one of the persistent and frustrating summer colds was coming. He swore again, knowing that he had to finish his work before he would be laid up in bed. He had a good staff, but they mainly worked during the picking and harvesting. At present, the four men and two women in his employ were walking the rows, clearing weeds, and repairing the racks. Only he could do this job. After blowing his nose on a handkerchief, Robert pulled on his gloves and resumed clearing the ground.

He was driving the tractor past a shallow dry wash when he felt the heavy machine dip as if it had hit a soft spot in the soil. But a moment later, it was again moving. A noise like a crack of lightning underground swept past him, but it went unheard in the diesel's roar.

The vintner made a broad turn, heading back along the edge of the cleared area. When he shifted into low gear, the engine noise subsided momentarily. Then he heard an ominous rumbling sound like rocks and gravel falling into a concrete pit. Robert turned off the ignition and let his ears adjust. The rumbling noise continued. He was about to climb down off the tractor when it lurched to one side. He clutched the steering wheel in both hands as the 5,000-kilogram machine dropped almost half a meter. He watched with horrified eyes as the ground rose around him. Then everything stopped.

Robert was ready to jump if the tractor continued to sink. But then the sound of falling stone subsided. Nothing else happened. With his heart racing, he started the engine and carefully nudged the accelerator pedal. The huge ribbed wheels found purchase until he was on firm soil again. Cutting the ignition, he climbed off. Wiping the beads of cold sweat from his forehead and cheeks, Robert regarded the wide circular depression in the earth. It looked like a bomb crater. He knew it was a sinkhole. He estimated it to be about twenty meters across and three deep. The weight of the tractor had probably cracked open a limestone cavern under the field. They were common in the region. Some were scores of meters deep. "*Merde,*" he said aloud, realizing how close he'd come to falling into his own grave. "I will have to fence off this area." He was relieved it was on the boundary of the area he'd planned to open. At least it wouldn't affect his plans. He kicked a large clod of dirt into the crater and watched as it came to rest at the bottom.

He took a swig of water from a canteen slung on the side of the tractor's seat. A few minutes later, his heart resumed its normal rhythm. He shook his head. It could have been worse. One farmer a few kilometers away had driven his brand-new tractor into an old underground ammunition dump from the First World War. Several live artillery shells had detonated, damaging the tractor and maiming the farmer.

Robert took a last look at the crater and surveyed the field around him. He wanted to get at least sixty more meters cleared before returning to the house. His only daughter, Fiona, would be arriving from Paris, and he wanted to see her, even though she would have her Italian accountant husband with her. Antonio didn't know a damned thing about winemaking, but he was good to Fiona. He was sure his daughter would put him to bed and make him rest. There would be no avoiding it. Yet, he loved the attention.

After blowing his nose again, Robert climbed back onto the tractor and started the engine. Then he let up the clutch and turned to attack another section.

Behind him, dirt clods and rivulets of soil continued to settle into the wide depression.

But André Robert was wrong. He hadn't broken into a limestone cavern. It was an underground stone cellar. Inside, the air was cold and dry, permeated with the musty scent of dust, age, and ancient death. Halfway down a long central hallway, one wall and several meters of the vaulted ceiling had collapsed in a broad landslide of broken stone.

After the last few pieces of shattered stone had come to rest on the dusty floor, no other sounds disturbed the black stillness. The dark cellar was again as silent as a crypt.

But now, something had changed. A faint warm breeze carrying the fragrance of grass and soil wafted through the black cellar. Fresh air stirred up the dust of ages.

Behind sealed doorways was the sound of breathing. Deep in the black cellar, an ancient predator had been disturbed from its millennia-long slumber.

CHAPTER I

AWAKENING

Slowly, almost reluctantly, Lucius began to awaken. He felt as though he were lying in icy water, rising slowly into warm air. He was first aware of his face. Nothing else seemed to exist but for his eyes, nose, and lips. The sensation was an ethereal presence spreading into his flesh. A faint breath of cool air tickled his eyelids and caressed his forehead and hair as if an old friend had passed nearby. His ears caught a soft sound down inside his chest. It was his heart heralding its presence with a living rhythm. Hot vital blood flowed in his arteries, veins, and capillaries. His joints awakened one at a time. Hips, elbows, knees, wrists, ankles, fingers, and toes stirred so slowly he could feel the quickening in every single knuckle. The ranks of joints awaited a command from his brain.

Lucius gingerly flexed the muscles of his jaw. Then he opened his eyes. There was nothing but utter blackness and this frightened him. He willed his right hand to move. It rose on the heavy arm, a towering pillar of unsteady flesh and bone. It was almost dead with weakness. The hand fell across his neck with a thud. He willed his fingers to crawl past his mouth to his eyes. A sharp pain proved his eyes were indeed open.

Am I blind? Then he remembered he had been in darkness when the Somnum began. *We need light,* he thought.

Then he heard the faint sound of breathing to his right.

He tried to reach out, but his arm was still weak. It fell on another body, prompting a grunt from the darkness. A hand grasped him with fervent desperation. "Lucius?"

Lucius replied in a pale whisper. "Yes. Marcus?" His tongue felt like old leather.

"Yes," said the voice from the blackness.

"Can you move?"

A grunt was his answer. "Not yet. My body is dead weight."

Marcus Titus was the strongest man Lucius had ever known, yet even he was as weak as a newborn lamb.

"It is the same with me," said another voice from Lucius's left. "I am so weak." That would be Septimus Deo Scipio.

"Ah, Septimus. You too." Lucius was beginning to feel almost normal. All his senses were coming alive.

"One of us should try to light a candle," said Marcus.

"You are welcome to try," Lucius said with a try at humor.

"As soon as I learn to where my legs have run off," his companion joked.

Weak laughs echoed from the darkness around them.

So the rest are in the same condition, Lucius realized. It made him feel less like an invalid. Then he heard footsteps past Septimus. *Someone has managed to stand. I hope he can reach the candles.* Then they heard a clatter and the sound of stone striking on metal. Suddenly a bright, searing flash caused many voices to cry out in pain. Lucius hadn't known his eyes were wide open. He squeezed them shut, waiting for the whirling stars in his head to disappear. He realized the blinding flash had been mere sparks from a flint.

"We have light, Sire," said another voice.

Lucius opened his eyes. Now he saw a candle flame. It illuminated the darkness like daylight.

"Well done, legionary," Lucius said. "Who are you?"

"Fabius Alexandrus, Sire," the man said. "Optio of Pilus Prior under Marius Vitellus."

Lucius heard another voice. "Good man, Alexandrus. You make us proud." That was Vitellus. After taking some deep breaths, Lucius lifted his head. It felt like a heavy stone atop his neck. Around him were many other men. Marcus, his laticlavius, or second-in-command, was smiling at him. "We have arisen from the pit, Sire," he said with a trace of his usual humor.

Lucius grinned. "It would appear so." Feeling like he weighed as much as a marble column, he set his hands on the wooden planks of the bunk. He felt a thick layer of coarse dust under his fingers. There should have been a linen mattress stuffed with straw, but all that remained was fragments and dust. How strange. He gripped one of the corner posts and placed his feet on the stone floor. Slowly he stood, feeling as if he were miles tall, horribly unwieldy. He willed his legs to stop shaking.

Lucius Cassius Aquilius, Legatus of Legio LIV, stood straight and steady. "My legionaries, we have risen."

A chorus of hoarse cheers greeted his ears. Now in his fortieth year, Lucius was tall with strong limbs and a solid chest. His deep-set brown eyes were intelligent and calculating. A square chin and high cheekbones, the legacy of his Northern Italian blood, made him the image of the handsome Roman officer. He scratched his head and was surprised at what he felt. His thick black hair, usually cropped in the short soldier's style, had grown down to his eyebrows and over his shoulders. He saw the same growth on his companions. They all had beards. "It appears we have been asleep for some time," he said.

Lucius surveyed their surroundings. They were in a large stone chamber about fifteen paces square. Thick columns supported a vaulted ceiling. Rows of tiered wooden bunks were set along the stone walls. Tiny pairs of glints revealed the eyes of dozens more men in the gloom. Their collective breath warmed the cold, stale air. On the floor along the walls were scores of tarnished bronze bowls. Inside each was a residue of a burned charcoal-like substance.

Alexandrus stood near a closed doorway. Next to him was a shelf with a bronze canister. Lucius knew it had held tallow candles, flint, and steel.

Marcus stood next to Lucius. The two men smiled at one another. He was a head taller than Lucius. His heavy forehead and strong chin framed the face of a warrior. The long dark brown hair made him look like a lion. The candlelight cast his muscular physique into sharp relief, making deep shadows on his bare arms. Marcus Titus had well earned his cognomen of "Ursus," or bear.

Septimus Deo had a thin, aesthetic face and high forehead. A narrow nose bisected brown eyes. He was a scholar, an anachronism in the Roman Army.

Lucius regarded their state of dress. They wore simple wool tunics ending above the knees. Once a deep wine-red, the wool was nearly black and very thin, almost tattered. On their feet were leather caligae laced up to the knee. The leather was as hard as wood and the thongs crumbled apart as they moved.

"It appears our impedimenta needs to be replaced," said Septimus with a wry smile.

Lucius nodded toward the thick wooden door. "We prepared for this. We will go and rouse the rest of the men. Vitellus, you are in command here."

"Yes, Sire," replied Vitellus. "I will see to it." Then he faced the others. "You heard our Legatus. Stand up like men." Then he walked to a doorway in the rear of the room. "You men in there. You have slept long enough. On your feet."

With the sound of shuffling feet and creaking wood, the legionaries stood. One man tried to stand, but the triple bunk fell apart with a sudden crash. He and two others untangled themselves from the dusty pile of broken wood. Another bunk fell, and then one more. The other legionaries rose to their feet, careful not to collapse any more bunks.

"That is odd," observed Septimus. "They were built to last an age." He and Marcus lit three candles. Lucius took one.

The door was set with massive iron hinges. Around the edge was a gasket made of thick leather. Marcus pulled the iron ring set into the face of the thick wood. At first, it resisted, but with a creak and groan, the door gave way and opened to reveal blackness beyond. After stepping through, they looked around. They were in a long hall wide enough for ten men to walk abreast. To their left was the base of a broad masonry stairway that ended at a solid stone wall. Every thirty paces on both sides of the hall were closed doorways.

"The air out here smells fresh," Marcus observed. "Not musty like in the chamber."

Lucius had also noted the clean air. "I feel a faint breeze."

Septimus reached the next door and shoved at the wood until it creaked open. He called for anyone to answer. A moment later they heard a weak voice. "Yes, Sire. I cannot see."

"Find candles and awaken the rest of your men," Septimus ordered. So they moved on and did the same in the following two rooms.

They found the fourth door ajar. It was eerily silent inside. The three candles revealed nothing but a dark room with a fetid odor filling the air. Lucius frowned and looked at the carved numerals on the lintel. Cohor. II Cento. V-VI.

"The Fifth and Sixth Centuries of Cohort Secundus," Lucius mumbled. "Where are they?"

Marcus stepped into the silent room. "They are here, Sire," the Laticlavus called out. His booming voice echoed off the stone walls.

Lucius went in, followed by Septimus. He recoiled at what he saw. On the bunks were moldering skeletons lying prone in neat rows as if for inspection. "What happened?"

"I do not know," Marcus said. He went to the door to the rear chamber.

Septimus examined the bones. "They appear to have been dead for ages."

Like the bunks, the legatus mused. Lucius looked at the neat rows of bowls on the floor along the walls. Fifty in this room, fifty more in the room Marcus had entered. Three thousand in the entire cellar. He remembered when they had begun the Somnum. He and his men had entered their chamber and tightly sealed the door. Each of the fifty bronze bowls on the floor had a wick set into the fibrous paste made from the strange water plant. "Light the wicks and lie down," he remembered saying to his men. In minutes the room had filled with thick, sweet-smelling smoke. Lucius grew drowsy as he told his men to inhale the smoke. "When we awaken from this Somnum, years will have passed. We will emerge and our attack will take our enemies by surprise. We will have our revenge at long last." Then there was only silence and darkness.

It had worked. The eccentric but brilliant alchemist's impossible scheme of putting them all to sleep for years had worked! He regarded the skeletons. Perhaps it had worked too well. "An age? I wonder how long it has been."

Septimus shook his head. "A hundred years at least."

Lucius wondered if a hundred years was enough time to turn a man into a pile of bones. The odor of putrefaction followed them from the death chamber.

Back in the hall, they heard voices. The light from several candles cast orange squares on the dusty stone floor.

Marcus rejoined them. "Eighty more are dead in the back room," he said, his face showing deep shock and anger.

"One hundred and sixty men dead," Lucius said bitterly. "Two entire centuria."

They found more rooms filled with skeletons. Lucius felt his frustration rising as the number of dead legionaries soared.

They reached the end of the hall. More than half of the sixty chambers had contained nothing but bunks of skeletons, but four rooms had held a different macabre scene. There was a long stretch of collapsed wall and broken stone. Only with difficulty could Marcus find his way into the first room. He saw the remains of dozens of crushed and smashed bodies under tons of fallen limestone. Sometime recently, their world had caved in and crushed the life out of them. Scratch at least three hundred more from the roll tablets.

Septimus went to make a count of the remaining men while Lucius and Marcus reached a vast storeroom. Lucius remembered the labor it had required to excavate the pit and build the huge cellar. His engineer, Corsicus Theodorus, had assured him it would withstand the test of time. The boast had proved true. Then Lucius realized that one of the crushed bodies was Theodorus.

There were dozens of long rows of standing wooden racks and shelves stacked with hundreds of tightly sealed bronze containers. Helmets, plate armor, shields, spears, swords, and other impedimenta lined the shelves. The metal had tarnished almost black.

Lucius picked up a helmet. He ran his fingers along the smooth brow-guard and cheek pieces. The leather lining was cracked and dry. Sliding a gladius from its scabbard, he tested the keen edge.

Marcus pried open a canister to reveal tightly rolled tunics and leather gear. "Ah, caligae. We can replace these old ones."

Lucius nodded. The orange candle flame glinted in his dark eyes. "All is well in here at least," he said with barely concealed bitterness.

Septimus stepped over to him. "Sire, I have the muster of the legion."

"Very well, Septimus Deo," Lucius said. "Tell me."

Septimus was unhappy to be giving the legatus bad news. He read from a wax tablet. "Cohorts Primus, Secundus, Quartus, Quintus, and Septimus are at partial strength with the loss of 985 men. Cohorts Tertius, Sextus, Octavus, Nomus, and Decimus are all dead. Our strength is now at 1,153 legionaries and officers."

Lucius knew it would be bad, but he had no idea the loss would be so devastating. Less than a third of the legion had survived. With an effort, he kept his shoulders from slumping.

Marcus stood at his side. His dark face showed the same shock and anger. Once numbering more than 4,800 armed and ready foot soldiers and officers, Legio LIV had been the finest legion ever assembled. Now, created for only one purpose, it was a shell of its former self. Down to five understrength cohorts, it was little more than a millaria.

Septimus continued. "I examined the rooms where we found only bones. It appears the doors had not been sealed tightly."

Lucius's eyes widened. "All those men lost because they had not closed the doors?"

The other man nodded soberly. "The smoke escaped before it could do its work. It was the same in every case."

The legatus expelled a long breath. "I see."

Marcus said, "The alchemist Gothicus Romulus told us the smoke had to be sealed in."

"I remember."

Septimus looked at his slate. "Cohort Quintus, under Primus Julius Plinus lost 332 officers and legionaries out of 480."

"Plinus," Lucius said with a scowl. "He was the hardest to convince. He did not truly believe the Somnum would work. Did he survive?"

Septimus shook his head. "He must have ignored the alchemist's orders."

"Yes," Lucius replied.

Septimus had more to tell. "We felt fresh air coming from the rooms which had collapsed. It must have happened very recently. It may be why we finally awoke."

"I see," Lucius said. "Have all officers meet here as soon as they can." Septimus moved off.

"Sire," said Marcus, "should we open the shaft?"

Lucius gave him a nod. "Yes. Have the engineers begin at once. I want a party of exploratories to scout the area." Then he shook his head. "We have lost so many, Marcus."

"We have, Lucius Cassius," Marcus said, using his legatus's name. They had been friends since they had been legionaries in Gallicae. "But we will prevail. Our cause lives on."

"Yes. It does. And the promise we made must be kept." No matter how many they'd lost, his legion would do as Lucius had vowed on that hot bloody summer day in Germania.

A short time later, the officers met at the archway leading to the storeroom. Lucius wore new caligae and a red tunic. A belt girded his waist with his badge of rank emblazoned on the buckle. He looked around at the officers of the five surviving cohorts. Next to him was the powerful Marcus. Beside him stood Septimus, and leaning on the wall to his left was Marius Vitellus. He was a Roman whose courage and daring had become a legend. In a running battle against rebellious Iberians, the barrel-chested Vitellus had led his troops into a throng of sword-waving warriors who outnumbered them three to one. Vitellus had charged at a dead run into the stunned enemy. In less than ten minutes, the rebels fled from the enraged Romans. Vitellus was decorated with the most favored of medals, the Insignia Triumphalia. He was the centurio of Pilus Prior of Cohort Primus. Vitellus's father had been a highly respected officer in Legio XVIII in Germania and one of Lucius's closest friends.

Past Vitellus was Centurio Cladius Atticus, a dark-skinned man of Sicilian blood. His black eyes glinted in the candlelight. Lucius had often felt those eyes boring into him as if he were being studied and probed for weaknesses. While Atticus was a fierce veteran fighter, Lucius knew from Vitellus that Atticus often boasted that he would be a better leader. But when they marched into Gallicae and began work on the cellar, Atticus had been there, doing his job. Now he was the senior surviving officer of Cohort Secundus.

Beside Atticus was a young officer named Pompaeius Sestus. His centurio had died during the Somnum. Sestus was younger than the other officers, having only been in the army for ten years. Like Vitellus, he had lost male relatives in Germania and lusted for revenge. His frank gaze was focused on Lucius.

Three more officers stood together. Brothers Regulus, Sirius, and Centaurus were known in the legion as the "Three Stars." They had joined Legio LIV as a group, asking that they be in the same cohort. They were inseparable and loyal to Lucius. Regulus and his younger brothers commanded the legion's superb archers. Lucius was glad they had survived.

"My loyal soldiers," Lucius began in a strong voice, "the time has come for us to break free from our self-imposed prison to reclaim our honor and that of the Empire. I know some years have passed, and Augustus will no longer be emperor. But I assure you the Imperium of Rome will be honored by our great deed. No matter how long it has been since we began the Somnum, we will seek the vengeance for which we have so long lusted."

Vitellus's face flushed with resolve at this.

Lucius continued. "We do not know what will be awaiting us above, but we shall deal with it as Roman soldiers. The world may be quite different from what we knew. But there are still enemies of Rome out there. We will reorganize into three cohorts. They will be under the command of Septimus Deo, Marius Vitellus, and Cladius Atticus. Organize the centuria to assure equal numbers of officers, legionaries, archers, medicii, engineers, and scouts."

Marcus caught his attention. "Will we march to Rheims? It is the capital of Gallicae Belgicae."

"No," Lucius said emphatically. "Rheims may have Roman governors who are aware that the army is not to cross the Rhenus River. We cannot risk being stopped even by our own countrymen." He paused. "We are, as from the beginning, on our own."

The assembled officers glanced at one another but made no protest.

"Sire," Vitellus asked, "how shall we deal with any Gauls we encounter?"

"A good question, Marius Vitellus," Lucius replied. He thought about how much the younger man resembled his father. "For now, all are to be avoided. We must use stealth to reach our goal. We do not do this out of cowardice," he said. "We have to be cautious. If we were at full strength, I would have no reservations about marching in daylight with our standard before us. That is no longer possible." Out of the corner of his eye, he saw Atticus shake his head. "You disagree, Atticus?"

The officer showed no embarrassment. "I do, Sire."

"Go on. You may speak freely." *For now*, Lucius didn't say.

"It is foolish to continue with our original plan. We have no chance of succeeding."

Vitellus and Marcus reacted strongly to this, but Lucius held up a hand. He knew what Marcus and Vitellus were thinking. They had lost fathers in Germania. "You took the Oath just as the rest of us. Now you wish to quit?"

"No, Sire," said Atticus. He saw the glowering faces of Vitellus and Marcus. "I only feel it is futile. A thousand men cannot do what an entire legion was to do."

Lucius's eyes narrowed. You gave your word. I will not tolerate any man who fails in his duty to our cause." His voice hardened. "Do I make myself clear?"

Atticus nodded. "You do, Sire. I meant neither disrespect to you nor our cause."

Lucius nodded. "We will do our duty to Rome and our fallen comrades. Even if we ultimately fail, it must never be said that Roman legionaries are not willing to die for their honor."

Atticus looked down at the floor. "I will follow your orders, Sire. I was only pointing out that we may no longer be able to complete our mission."

"Nothing has changed, Atticus," Lucius said flatly. "You are still an officer in the Roman Army. Your duty comes first. Is there anything else?"

Septimus cleared his throat. "Sire, I took an inventory of our vittles."

Lucius could tell from his friend's expression the news was bad. He sighed. "What is left?"

"Very little. The grain, nuts, and fruit are completely decayed."

Lucius gritted his teeth. "Is there anything left?"

"All the hard bread survived," Septimus said with a trace of humor. The others smiled too. The hard bread could be counted upon to last years, even if it was almost inedible when fresh.

"Very well. We will forage for food on the march. There are many crops in this region."

"It will not be easy to conceal the foraging of more than a thousand men," said Septimus.

"I realize that. We will travel at night and conceal ourselves during daylight."

Then he looked back at the officers around him. "We have lost many men, and much time has passed. But nothing else has changed. We have our duty. The entrance will be opened and scouts will go out. Resume your preparations."

The assembled officers saluted and left.

A team of engineers was working at the top of the stairs, removing the heavy stones that sealed the tunnel to the outside world. A beefy Tuscan named Arcturius was the legion's senior surviving engineer. He knew which blocks had to be removed first to prevent a collapse, or worse, permanent sealing of the tunnel.

"I am amazed that Gothicus's plan worked," Marcus said to Lucius as they watched the engineers at their work.

"So am I," Lucius replied. "He was a peculiar old man, but his alchemical skills were beyond reproach." He glanced down the long hallway.

"I wonder how long it has been," Marcus said, voicing what Lucius was thinking.

"I wish I knew. Septimus thinks it may be more than a hundred years."

Marcus sighed. "It was the plan all along to sleep for many years." Then he smiled. "Perhaps I will meet my great-great-great-grandson when we return to Rome."

Lucius laughed. "It would help if you had married and sired sons first."

The tall man grinned. "Ah, but how would the ladies of Rome ever have forgiven me if I had?"

Lucius thought of the rooms filled with bones. He was still angered. Over three thousand of his men dead. "A great injustice so many were lost to the mere failure to seal a door. What a waste."

They watched as the next shaped block of stone was loosened and levered aside to the stairs. "I wonder what we shall find up there?" Marcus was trying to distract Lucius from his anger.

"A different world but a Roman one," the legatus said.

"Of course, a Roman one! What other world could it be?"

The two old friends shared another laugh.

Even with twenty strong men bending to the task, it was two hours before the final huge block was ready for removal. Arcturius called for Lucius. "Sire," he said with a voice that echoed down the stone hall, "we are ready to pull the last block. Shall we proceed?"

Lucius replied with a nod. "Yes, do so now. We must make haste. The exploratories are ready."

"As you command, Sire." Arcturius motioned for the men to begin. As each block had been removed, it was added to form a broad ramp with a flat landing beside the last block.

An incredible feat of engineering, Lucius thought with pride, even for Romans.

Arcturius pried out a thick keystone, and the huge block was levered onto the landing. Stooping, he entered the tunnel. Just inside, the smooth dressed stone walls gave way to hard-packed soil entwined with dense roots. He thrust a pry bar into the dirt face and twisted. A few clods fell away. He struck again and again, each time dislodging more dirt. Then with a stiff jab, he finally broke through the wall of soil. When Arcturius pulled the bar free, he felt a cool breeze of fresh air on his face. He turned back and said, "We are through, Sire!"

Another man came to help, and in a few minutes, they pulled a large mass of soil out of the wall before them. It broke away and fell onto the stairs, scattering clods across the floor. In minutes, they had dug an opening large enough for a man to duck through.

Fresh air flowed into the cellar. Hundreds of legionaries inhaled the sweet air of the outside world.

Lucius climbed the stairs with Marcus and Septimus behind him. When he ducked to peer out through the narrow dirt tunnel, he saw sunlight. The low sun warmed his face. It felt like a caress from a woman's warm hand. The sun's bright disk was low in the western sky, silhouetting a row of evergreens on a low ridge. It appeared to be late afternoon. His companions came up behind him. Together they inhaled the fragrant scent of fresh air and basked in the warmth from the sun. The outside world was before them for the first time since they had begun the Somnum. Legio LIV Vindicta had at last awakened.

CHAPTER II

LOVE AND WAR

"Thank you for your time, Mister Braden," the colonel said pleasantly. "I feel a lot better now."

"Not at all, Colonel," Alex Braden replied. He stood and walked the Army officer to his office door. "These things happen in any line of work. Sometimes we need a little help. The Army doesn't need another drug scandal."

The colonel nodded. "Yeah, this was keeping me awake at night. I could see my entire career finished, and all because of a simple bottle of pain pills."

Braden grinned. "Just remember to keep the prescription and receipt next time you plan to travel to Amsterdam."

The colonel checked his wristwatch. "Wow, it's later than I thought. Sorry to keep you at your desk so long."

"No problem," Braden said amiably. "I'm pretty much done for the day. Take care, Colonel." The two men shook hands. Braden stood at the door for a moment, watching the officer walk down the hallway of the NATO Legal Services Department. Alex Braden was average in stature with an athletic build from hours of swimming at the public pool near his apartment. His summer tan emphasized a handsome angular face and square jawline below sandy hair and blue eyes.

He went back to his desk, where he quickly wrote his closing report on the computer.

This had been his last appointment of the week. It was late Thursday afternoon and he was taking Friday off.

He glanced out the window. The sun was touching the roofline of six-story buildings to the west. The European Weather Channel had forecast fine weather over northern Europe, perfect for the three-day weekend with his girlfriend, Ann. It would be good to get out of the city for a while.

A graduate of the University of Maryland Law School with degrees in history and criminal investigation, Braden began his career as Legal Affairs Assistant at the American Consulate in Bonn, Germany. Two years later, he transferred to Paris.

Hard work and a lucky break were responsible for his posting as a military legal investigator at the North Atlantic Treaty Organization Headquarters in Brussels, Belgium. It was by far the most challenging and rewarding job he'd ever known.

Now a month past his thirty-second birthday, he spoke fluent French, Flemish, and passable German. He investigated crimes committed on and by American military personnel, gathering information for the U.S. Army's Criminal Investigation Division. He most often took cases that crossed international borders. To this end, Braden possessed the coveted status of diplomatic immunity. Occasionally he worked on cases involving drugs, rape, murder, theft, and espionage, any of which could awaken the evil hydra of an "international incident." Those two words were as unwelcome at NATO as "malpractice lawsuit" was to a doctor.

He tapped a ballpoint pen on his desk, mentally cataloging what he had to do before leaving. After making notes and signing off on the colonel's file, he slid it into his "out" tray. He typed an email to central files, but the network was balky and refused to accept the "send" command. "Crap," he snarled under his breath. "Here we go again." He gave up and logged off the system.

He looked around his office to be sure everything was in order before locking up. Behind him was a tall bookcase with neat rows of legal texts on international and European law, forensics, criminal investigation, the Manual of Courts-Martial, and the Uniform Code of Military Justice. To his right was a window that overlooked the parking lot two floors below. It wasn't much of a view, but some offices had no windows at all. The floor was bare wood, and the simple furniture showed its more than three decades of use. But he had a comfortable leather chair he liked to lean back in while thinking.

Against the wall next to the door was a glass-fronted cabinet containing his display of military antiques, items he'd collected since his boyhood. American Civil War buttons, bullets, and belt buckles rested next to German bayonets and helmets from the Second World War.

Since being in Europe, he'd added items from the Napoleonic Wars, including a French cavalry saber.

In the center was his pride and joy, a small bronze disk about the size of a silver dollar. He'd found it in a curio shop a year before. The shop owner hadn't known what it was. Yet Alex Braden, an amateur military historian, bought the lion's head emblem from a Roman centurion's belt for the astonishing sum of thirty euros. Now it rested in a place of honor on deep red velvet. Sometimes Braden gazed at the ancient disk, thinking of the two thousand years since a Roman soldier had carried it into battle. If Braden could have one wish, it would be to go back in time and roam freely among the great armies of the ancient world.

After a last look around, he turned off the lights and locked the door.

The Legal Services Department numbered fifteen attorneys, five investigators, twenty paralegals, and clerical staff. Some had administrative areas of responsibility, while others worked on cases in specific NATO-member countries.

Braden's investigative work with American military personnel often crossed administrative borders as well as national ones.

Their boss, a former Texas state prosecutor named Jonathan Howard, had been with NATO since the First Gulf War in 1991. Fair and good-natured, Howard had a well-deserved reputation for always being on the job. He worked six days a week and missed nothing in his domain.

Braden entered Howard's outer office and greeted the executive assistant. "Hey, Charlene. Ready for the weekend?"

Charlene Myers, a beautiful lady of twenty-eight, with brains and skill in even more quantity, smiled at him while typing on her computer. "I sure am, Alex. I know you're taking tomorrow off and going away with Ann."

Braden smiled. Charlene never forgot a name or a birthday, even those of parents and children. "Yeah, we're meeting at our favorite café, then we're off for a weekend in the country. Is the boss in?" He looked toward the closed inner door.

"Yeah, but he's in a meeting with Joan and the secretary-general."

"Wow," Braden said, impressed. "The secretary's in there? I'm surprised I didn't hear about it." Howard frequently had to meet with ambassadors and government officials. The secretary-general of NATO, a taciturn and serious Frenchwoman named Louisa Rochambeau, didn't often darken the Legal Department's doorways.

Charlene didn't look up from her typing. Her fingers were literally a blur on the keyboard. "It's about Germany."

"Oh. Well, Colonel Parker is in the clear. I confirmed the pills were prescription and have his wife's doctor's statement to back it up. I was going to email it to John and Major Martinez at CID, but the server's giving me trouble again."

Charlene sighed. "You too, huh? I'll get IT on it."

"Thanks."

Her fingers continued their dizzying dance.

Incredible, Braden thought. *She's a multitasking poster girl.*

Charlene stopped typing and did a few quick isometric exercises, stretching her arms over her head and spreading them wide. The taut fabric of her white blouse stretched over her bosom.

Braden tried not to look, but Charlene's figure made it about as easy as ignoring a speeding train when you are tied to the track.

"Alex, I do need to wrap things up, so could you be a lamb and beat it?" Her china-blue eyes flashed with mirth as if she knew damned well he'd been looking and not minding at all.

Braden smiled sheepishly. "I just like chatting with you." She was a favorite at NATO.

"I know, tiger. But get lost, please?" She smiled warmly.

"Okay, I'm history." He grinned and reached for the doorknob. "You have a great weekend."

"You too. Tell Ann I want to go shopping next time she's in town."

"Got it. See you Monday."

Braden lived in a modest apartment outside Brussels, not far off the highway that led to the Waterloo battlefield. Pulling off his tie, he threw it and his coat on the back of the couch and went into the kitchen for a beer. He preferred American lagers and had arranged for a friend in the quartermaster's office to obtain a case of Samuel Adams for him each month. Braden had saved the sergeant a lot of money on a rental car accident. He twisted off the cap from his one precious bottle for the day. His voicemail held a message from his mother in Baltimore, telling him to call her during the weekend. Another one was from Ann, reminding him about their meeting at the café.

"Sheesh. As if I'd forget," he said aloud. A glance at his watch told him he still had an hour. The café was only a fifteen-minute walk.

The television offered nothing of worth, so he picked up Stephen Ambrose's *D-Day: June 6, 1944.* In a few minutes, he was engrossed in a gripping narrative on the battle for Normandy in World War Two.

Forty minutes later, Braden set the book aside and stood. He put the beer bottle in a recycling bin by the back door and made a quick trip to the bathroom. After donning a sports jacket, he was out the door. Outside the sky was a cool rose-pink as the mid-summer sun settled on the western horizon over the old city skyline. The spires and steep rooflines of the town always reminded him of an old Grimm's fairy tale village. He enjoyed walking in Brussels, thinking of its history. Everyone in the western world had marched through Belgium over the centuries, both friend and foe. The Gauls, Romans, Celts, Vikings, Saxons, English, and Germans had all set foot on Belgian soil over the last two thousand years.

"And now it's down to one lone Yank," he said quietly.

Ann Hamilton was at their usual table when he arrived a few minutes late. He leaned over and kissed her cheek while handing her a single red rose. She held the crimson flower to her nose. "Mmm. Nice."

Braden settled into the chair across from her. "How are you, honey?"

"Fine. What's the rose for? Are you feeling guilty about something?" Her London accent fit somewhere between Oxford and public school.

"Guilty? Moi? No, I just felt like it. I was passing the florist stand."

"Ah, so that's why you're late," she said.

"Yeah. I figured I'd make myself late and make up for it at the same time."

She grinned. "Silly bugger. I already ordered for us. Thursday special is fish and chips, rounded off with some good Bass Ale. Sound good?"

"I can live with that," he said with a smile. "It sounds wonderful right about now. So what was work like this week?"

Ann expelled a disgusted snort. "Don't get me started. His royal majesty Sir Lee Patterson is on the bloody warpath again. He told me he expects a twenty-five percent increase in new client accounts over the next six months." Her nostrils flared. "Twenty-five bloody percent, Alex. My God, that's more than three hundred new clients, both business and holiday." Then, with a shake of her head, she muttered, "Almost makes me wish I'd stayed on as a paramedic. At least that job gave me some satisfaction when I helped save a life."

Ann had once been an emergency medical technician in one of East London's most violent districts. She worked on drug overdoses and gunshot victims almost every night. When despair of the job had gotten to her, she began attending night school to become a travel agent. Ann now held the post of senior marketing associate for the London office of Excalibur Travel Group. Twice a month she met with managers in Brussels, Bonn, Hamburg, Paris, and Rotterdam. It gave her and Braden plenty of opportunities to see each other.

"Wow," he said. "Can you do it?" He knew there wasn't much Ann Hamilton couldn't do once she took on a new challenge. She just had to vent first.

"Puh-leeze," she said, rolling her eyes. "I just have to come up with some new adverts and campaigns. It'll be bloody hard work, but yes, love, I can do it." While Ann was well-educated, some of the slang from her early years still came out in her speech. It was one of the things Braden loved about her.

The waiter distributed the plates heaped with battered whitefish and steaming hot chips. Despite his years in Europe, Braden still had trouble calling what he'd always known as French fries as chips. When in Rome.

He picked up a bottle of ketchup and poured a generous amount on his fish and a large dollop at the side of the fries. "Does that mean you'll have less free time?"

Ann took a sip from her beer. "Not on your life, my love. I can handle it. I'll not let this ridiculous directive take my precious free time away."

"I'm glad to hear that."

He studied her while she poured malt vinegar on her fish and sprinkled salt on the chips. Ann was a few centimeters over a meter and a half tall with long, deep golden blonde hair tied in a ponytail. Her heart-shaped face, which made her seem far younger than her twenty-nine years, framed lovely cocoa-brown eyes, a cute bud of a nose, and soft lips. She'd come directly from the office, so she wore a deep red suit jacket, dark blue slacks, and an open-collared white blouse. Under this was a perfect body with full breasts and wide hips supported by two shapely legs atop ten carefully painted toes.

Braden had met Ann in Paris nearly three years previously at a party thrown by a mutual friend. The random meeting had changed his life. They'd been in love ever since. Shortly after coming under the spell of Ann Hamilton, he'd heard of an opening at the NATO Legal Services Department. He began the paperwork and clearances to join NATO. Six months later came the welcome news that he was accepted as an investigator for the department.

He finished his fries and looked longingly at her plate. He was still hungry. "So, what have you got planned for the weekend?" He stole a chip from her plate and popped it into his mouth.

"You'll love this one," she said, slapping his hand.

Her connections and discounts gave her access to interesting and fun vacations. They'd boated down the Danube, driven across the Alps, and spent two weeks touring wineries in the Loire Valley.

"What is it?"

Ann shook her head. A blonde wisp fell across her forehead. She blew it away. "You'll see. I have it all set. You just drive."

His ever-active curiosity was immediately alert. "Can you give me a hint?"

Her brown eyes narrowed as if she were deciding what to say. "Let's just say you'll get to meet up with some men in armor."

He was intrigued. "Armor? What kind?"

She raised her eyebrows. "That's all I'm going to say."

"Okay. I'll wait. Want another beer?"

Her reply was a nod, and he waved to the waiter. The night was just beginning.

Flanius Plutonius was a veteran scout, having served in a legion in Gallicae for ten years. He and his companions wore only the tunic, haversack, and belt. To minimize noise, they wore no armor. But each man carried a gladius.

"Remember," Lucius cautioned them, "we do not know what you will find up there." His dark eyes looked longingly at the indigo sky through the rough opening. "Avoid contact with the Gauls. Scout and learn, find the roads and rivers. We need food and water so locate farms and livestock." Then his voice became hard. "If anyone sees you, kill them immediately."

Plutonius, a slim but firmly muscled native of Sicily, saluted and led the exploratories up the stairs. His heart pounded. He'd hated the eternal blackness and deathly stillness underground. *Like being dead*, he thought with a shudder. He ducked through the dirt tunnel to emerge on open ground. Plutonius took a deep breath as his men joined him. He looked around. A crescent moon hung like a familiar sentinel to the east. He saw they were in a deep vale thickly overgrown by tall grass and dotted with large trees. To the right was a low ridge crested by a neat row of pine trees. Behind them was a vineyard with acres of grapevines on tall wooden racks. A sigh passed Plutonius's lips as he remembered the taste of sweet wine.

In the center of the narrow valley ran a small stream slowly meandering among the trees and grass. There was a wood and metal bench near the water's edge. "Junius Crassius, go tell the legatus there is water here." The man ran back to the tunnel. He and the others thirstily drank water from cupped hands. Once they were refreshed, Plutonius looked at the sky. It was a deep cobalt blue sprinkled with stars. He turned until he found Polaris, the North Star. Then he found Sirius. It wasn't quite to its zenith. "It appears to be before midnight. I think it must be summer. We have hours until dawn." He ordered the men to spread out and climb the ridge. They should be able to see some distance from the ridgeline. When he reached the crest, Plutonius hunkered down. A road bisected a shallow valley of cultivated land. Crassius was beside him. "Look at that." He pointed west. Plutonius realized what his companion was indicating. From nearly north to south, the entire sky was strangely bright. He remembered seeing a comet that had remained in the sky for weeks when he was a boy. It had been a brilliant white and cast distinct shadows at night. He pulled a wax tablet and stylus from his haversack. The road ran nearly northeast to southwest. He drew a simple map showing the road and valley. "Crassius, come with me. The rest of you stay here and keep watch." Plutonius led the way down the slope to the roadway. He looked in both directions where it curved away to follow the winding valley and saw no one. Then he examined the road itself.

Plutonius had built and marched on roads all over the Empire. He was well aware of the best that Romans were capable of building. But this road was strange. The surface was some sort of dry, dark gray paste-like substance with gravel embedded in it. He supposed the Empire had made some advances in road building since the legion had begun the long Somnum.

A large sign was posted at the side of the roadway, bearing letters and characters. It read:

Reims 41 Km.

Epernay 75 Km.

He frowned. He recognized the name Reims. It was the largest city in Gallicae Belgicae, the seat of the Roman governor. He copied the markings on the tablet and returned his attention to the sign. It was very smooth and flat metal, like a mirror in a bathhouse. It was painted an odd white that seemed to catch the starlight. The post was also metal. How could anyone, even the Empire, afford to use such a precious resource for such a simple purpose? Metal was used for weapons, armor, tools, and the like.

Suddenly a distant rumble filled the air.

"Something is coming!" Crassius hissed sharply.

In an instant, the white sign was as brilliant as the sun. Plutonius cringed in shock. He spun to look down the road. A blazing white light stabbed his eyes. The two legionaries were dazzled by its intensity. Plutonius drew his gladius and motioned for Crassius to follow him into a ditch at the side of the road. The wave of sound approached like a thousand charging horses. Yet for all his bravery, Plutonius was shaking with fear. Two blinding white orbs like pieces of the sun were bearing down on him. He prayed to Apollo for strength and held up his gladius, prepared to do battle with the oncoming beast.

Then with a rush of roiled hot air that sent the dust flying and trees shaking, the thing had passed. The rumble receded with two glaring red eyes diminishing and growing smaller as the immense beast roared on down the road. Crassius was also stunned at what they'd seen. They shook the dust and dirt from their hair and stood. "What in the name of the gods was that?"

Crassius had no answer. It had been as big as a building and moved with unbelievable speed. And on the side had been words.

Moet et Chandon Champagne.

Meanwhile, groups of legionaries filled their bronze water flasks from the stream. They climbed the hill and picked as many grapes as they could carry. Deep purple dawn backlit the vast rows of grapevines as they finished.

Lucius called for Arcturius. "Gather planks from one of the doors and use them to conceal the entrance when Plutonius returns. We will have to wait out the day."

Plutonius and his team arrived just as the sun's edge crested the hills to the east. As the engineers worked to conceal the tunnel, the scout gave his report. Lucius and the rest of his officers listened with rapt attention as they heard about the new world outside. Plutonius described the massive noisy beast that had almost caught them. He knew it was not a living creature, but it had rattled him. He would not admit this to his commander. A veteran never admitted fear.

"It was not pulled by horses," he said. "It moved much faster than any horse could run at full gallop."

The officers exchanged looks of surprise as Plutonius described what had happened next. "Then a smaller four-wheeled vehicle approached at the same speed. It was no larger than a wagon but appeared to be clad in armor."

Lucius frowned. "And it had no horses hitched to it?"

"No, Sire," the scout said. "Nothing."

"What did you do after that?"

"We saw many lights of farms and small towns." Plutonius gestured to the tablet in Septimus's hand. He continued. "Beyond the ridge, the land flattened out, and we kept to the cover of trees. Finally, we found a large farm with buildings." He went on to describe the house, which had been painted white with perfectly square glass windows. "The lights were strange, not like fires or lamps. They were white and did not flicker."

Lucius glanced at Marcus, knowing what his friend was thinking. The world had changed considerably.

"Near the farmhouse was a large chariot like we saw on the road. I realized it was a mode of transport. It also had glass windows. It was clad in metal and very smooth to the touch. At one end, there was heat, as if it held fire. It rested on four black wheels of a material like hard tar."

"And that smell of the chariot," Crassius prompted.

Plutonius nodded. "Yes. It was like the air near Vesuvius when it is alive, a sooty unpleasant odor. We found a dump near the farm with large covered bins. They were full of food slops."

"What kind?" Septimus inquired.

"Old food, eggshells, and fruit peels," Plutonius replied, reaching into his haversack, retrieving some stiff paper items, and handing them to Lucius. "Things like this."

Lucius examined one in the candlelight. It was a red cup almost large enough to insert his hand. An oily vegetable scent clung to the inside. On one side was a symbol that appeared to be a yellow double arch.

He handed it to Septimus and told Plutonius to continue.

"The terrain to the east was hilly. Not much in the way of good cover, however. But we could not see any great distance."

"That is a concern," said Septimus. "We need cover in daylight."

Lucius ate some grapes while he thought this over. "A civilization that armors its vehicles has to be at war, and the only conceivable enemy must be Rome. We are far behind enemy lines."

"We might march only in the night and dig pits for the day," Marius Vitellus said. "And we can gather brush to conceal ourselves." Vitellus was wise enough to be cautious in an unknown land. His father's death in Germania had taught him that.

Lucius nodded again. "We will be cautious until we reach our goal. Even at our best pace of twenty-four miles, it will take many days, ah, nights of marching," he said, catching himself.

Plutonius reached for the map and pointed out possible routes. "This valley showed the least habitation, Sire. I would be honored to guide the legion on the march."

Lucius smiled. "Well done, Flanius Plutonius. Get some rest. We will be leaving once the sun has set again."

"Thank you, Sire." Plutonius saluted and took his leave.

While the legion prepared for the march, a dozen men complained of feeling dizzy and weak. The Medicus, or medical orderly, told them to rest in a chamber near the storeroom. Later, a legionary went to check in on a friend. A minute later, he called for the medicus. The orderly entered. His eyes grew wide in horror when he looked at the man on the nearest bunk. Instead of a robust, healthy soldier, he saw a man in the last moments of life. Sputtering with wheezing gasps, the man's hands trembled violently. Suddenly his chest heaved, and a long exhalation signaled the life ebbing away.

"What happened, Medicus?" the first man asked after seeing his friend die.

"I do not know," the orderly said, examining the dead man. The skin had a gray pallor like an old, weathered statue. The other sleeping men were in nearly the same condition. Another died. It was terrifying to watch.

The orderly found Lucius in the storeroom with Marcus. They turned at his approach.

"Sire, forgive me for interrupting you."

Lucius saw that something was wrong. "Yes, what is it?"

"I have looked in on the men who were stricken, Sire," he began. "They are nearly all dead. I do not understand why."

"I see," Lucius replied in a voice tinged with resignation. Around them were hundreds of legionaries collecting their marching gear and weapons. *How many will be left when we reach our goal*, he wondered. *Will we reach it?*

Marcus sighed. "I think we had better accept that we will lose more men this way. We have tempted the gods for too long."

Lucius sighed. "I do not think there is anything we can do to stop this. We are in a race and time is no longer our friend."

CHAPTER III

EMERGENCE

Arcturius levered a board aside and looked outside. He saw the last rosy tint of the sunset beyond the ridge to the west. It was time to leave. The sound of hundreds of legionaries collecting their equipment echoed in the storeroom and down the hallway. Every man wore new tunics and leather gear. The caligae were stiff but strong. The legionaries helped one another don their armor.

The curved plates of iron hinged and riveted to flexible leather straps covered them from neck to waist, making them look like metal armadillos.

Marcus adjusted Lucius's shoulder plates. "The metal has tarnished almost black. It will make us harder to see." He tied the last leather thong.

"Yes," said Lucius. His armor was ornate as befitted his rank. Strapped to his shins were bronze greaves. "I must have lost weight. It is very loose." He waggled his shoulders to make the armor fit more comfortably.

Marcus smiled. "I can afford to, but Septimus is so thin he may be no more than bones before we—" he broke off, realizing what he'd said.

Lucius pretended not to notice and fitted his helmet on his head. Then he tied the hinged cheek pieces under his chin. "This armor is far better than what we wore in Germania," he said, running his hand over the faded red horsehair crest. Marcus's white crest had turned a dingy gray. Lucius picked up his gladius from the shelf and slid the long blade from its scabbard. There were nicks all along its length, but the edges were straight and sharp. He remembered the day the old blacksmith Vulcanus had given it to him. The sword had been with him in every campaign and battle from Gallicae to Germania.

Marcus watched his friend. "That gladius has seen victory and defeat. Perhaps it will soon see victory again."

"Yes," said Lucius, looking at his reflection in the smooth blade. *You will taste barbarian blood again, I promise you.* Then he resumed putting on his gear. He pried open a large container with his name on the rim and pulled out a leather haversack. Inside were two codexes, one large and bound in leather and a smaller one with an embroidered fabric cover. It had belonged to his wife, Livia. He held it for a long moment, seeing the dried dark brownish stains on the cover. It was his most prized possession. Also inside the haversack was a small carved wooden figure of a legionary. Then with a sharp pang of emotion, he remembered his little son, Cornelius, also murdered in Germania with Livia. Then he returned them to the haversack along with a ration of hard bread and grapes. Lastly, he fitted a thick belt around his waist. Long metal-studded leather strips hung down from the belt, covering his groin. A water flask and short double-edged knife called a pugio rested on his left hip.

Lucius was ready. "Come, Marcus. The world awaits." He walked through the masses of fully outfitted legionaries and nodded to them as he passed. In addition to armor, they hung dark brown wool blankets over their shoulders. While some had spits, cooking pans, or utensils, others hefted pick-like entrenching tools and shovels. Every man carried two pila, the spear of the Roman Army. Arcturius and his men each slung a heavy coil of rope over their shoulders.

Marcus chuckled. "It appears we are back to being Marius's Mules again."

Lucius grinned, remembering the term for a legionary in the army of Gaius Marius a hundred years before. The former consul had done away with the cumbersome and slow baggage trains that accompanied the legions on campaigns. Forced to carry all their gear, the legionaries began derisively referring to themselves as mules. "It brings back memories of our training days under Spathus. He was a tyrant about loading us up on a route march."

"Do not remind me," Marcus said. "Many times I thought of taking that cursed vitis stick from him and—" He grinned. "Well, you know what I mean."

"It was a common wish," Lucius said, still grinning, "but he did build excellent and strong legionaries."

Lucius felt pride as he surveyed the men around him. Then he saw the three brothers surrounded by several dozen legionaries holding long-bows. "Regulus, I am pleased that many of our archers survived."

"They are the elite, Sire," said Regulus. He was taller than his brothers but had the same dark brown hair and heavy chin. His arms, like those of the other archers, were thick and muscled. "We are ready. We have extra bows and strings. The yew wood is still strong."

Gaius Julius did well by bringing the skill of archery from Britannia, Lucius thought. "Take twice your usual issue of arrows. We will need them."

"I will see to it," said Regulus.

Then Marcus spoke. "My concern is our scutum. How will we conceal them?"

Lucius regarded the many deeply curved shields of thick wood. They were tall enough to reach a man's elbow. They were painted bright red with gold wings and thunderbolts radiating out from a heavy metal boss in the center. Emblazoned across the center of each scutum were the words *LEG.LIV VDCTA.*

"They are very vivid."

"The men need the shields for protection," Lucius said. "And they proclaim who and what we are. Have the legionaries carry them across their backs under the blankets." He called to Arcturius. "Conceal the entrance after we depart. We must erase all evidence of our having been here."

"It will be done, Sire," said Arcturius.

Marcus looked toward the stairway. "I think we are in for some very astounding discoveries."

"But none a Roman Legion cannot handle," Lucius declared.

Marcus was a veteran of over a dozen battles. He looked at his friend and commander. "No, nothing a legion cannot handle." Then in a whisper, "Except we are no longer a full legion."

Legatus Lucius Cassius Aquilius stood halfway up the stairs and smiled at the sight of his legion. Neat ranks of over eleven hundred fully armed and armored legionaries filled the entire length of the hallway from wall to wall. Their helmets glinted dully in the candlelight. The barbed spears looked like the stiff fur on a warthog's back.

The legion was reorganized into three new cohorts of 370 men each. They were named Mars, Jupiter, and Apollo. Septimus was Primus Ordanes of Cohort Mars, while Marius Vitellus commanded Cohort Jupiter. Atticus led Apollo at the rear.

The aquilifer, a veteran named Quintus, was standing beside Lucius, holding the legion's standard. The wooden shaft was topped with a golden eagle whose talons gripped a wreath encompassing the *imago* of Emperor Augustus.

For a moment, Lucius regarded the standard. As a young legionary, he had fought in battle against rebelling Celts who had killed the aquilifer. Using his scutum and gladius, Lucius thrust himself into the mass of barbarians and killed the one who had taken the standard, then fought his way back into the Roman ranks.

He had earned the honorific of Aquilius, meaning "Savior of the Eagle."

Lucius watched as the engineers removed the planks from the entryway. He addressed his men. "We are all here for one reason, my faithful legionaries," he began. "I am proud of every one of you who has sacrificed so much for the honor of Rome. We are fewer in number, but that means a greater share of glory will be yours."

Every man stood more erect at this praise.

"A long time ago," he said in a somber voice, "we made a pledge to those we lost. They cry out from their graves for revenge. Our enemies do not know we are coming, and we will attack and destroy them without mercy."

Several legionaries thrust their pila into the air. Lucius saw the fervor in their eyes.

"Our journey will be one of hard marching and unknown danger, but as Romans, we can overcome anything. I chose you because I wanted men I knew would kill without fear, without hesitation, without remorse." Then he held his arms out wide and said in a firm voice, "What will you do when you meet the enemy?"

The legionaries shouted as one: "Destroy them!" The sound echoed off the stone walls like a physical force. Lucius's heart thumped hard beneath his armor. They must have heard that in Rome. The legionaries and officers chanted a single word over and over. "*Vindicta! Vindicta! Vindicta!*"

Lucius drew his gladius and pointed it at the dark blue sky beyond the entryway. "Then let us abandon this prison. Go forth, Legio Fifty-four! Reclaim our honor and victory for Rome!"

Charlotte Renaud waited impatiently in the dark by a narrow country road near her father's farm outside of the village of Rethel. Every few seconds, she looked down the road hoping to see the headlamp of Stefan's motorcycle.

"He should have been here twenty minutes ago," she said, angry and eager. She had waited until her parents, typically early-to-bed types, were fast asleep before climbing out her bedroom window and ducking through the thick hedge that surrounded her house. Charlotte had black hair and wide brown eyes. Her slim figure was clad in jeans and a blue peasant blouse. She never wore a bra when she went out to meet Stefan.

Her father had forbidden Charlotte to date boys until she was eighteen. That was intolerable to the popular and pretty fifteen-year-old. Most of her friends from school had been dating since they were fourteen, for God's sake. And here she was, having to creep out in the middle of the night to see Stefan. And as for being told never to let a boy touch her body under any circumstances, that was just medieval. She was old enough to make her own choices. But where the hell was he? She checked her watch again.

Then she heard the familiar purr of the BMW motorcycle. "It's about time," she said, knowing he was as horny as she.

Stefan Barat stopped his gleaming black motorcycle beside her and grinned. His white teeth and blond hair shone in the starlight. He wore jeans and a black T-shirt. "I'm sorry to be late, Char," he said over the hum of the motor. "My parents took their time about going to bed."

"I have been waiting forever," she pouted. "I was ready to go back home. Maybe I will anyway."

His eyes roamed over the smooth curves of her untethered breasts under the blouse. "Please, Char. I am sorry."

Then she smiled. "Okay. Let's go." She straddled the seat behind Stefan and wrapped her arms around his firm torso.

"As you wish, my princess," he replied and drove slowly down the road.

Charlotte had met Stefan at a fast-food place in town where she and her friends gathered after school. He was three years older than her, already out of school and working at a motorcycle repair shop. His world-wise charm, devil-may-care attitude, and good looks won Charlotte's young heart. Within a month, they had discovered the forbidden joys of sex and began sneaking out at night to make love in the country. No one knew of their illicit nocturnal trysts. But if word ever got out, her father would probably shoot Stefan and send her to a convent.

The motorcycle's speed made Charlotte's black ponytail whip around in a tiny imitation of its namesake as she held on to her boyfriend. A short time later, they reached a small clearing at the edge of a thick pine grove. After turning off the BMW's motor, Stefan looked around. Overhead, the tall evergreens eclipsed the stars like black sentinels. "Looks like the coast is clear," he said. The air was warm and fragrant with the loamy scent of grass and soil. He unrolled a blanket on the spongy grass. Before he could say anything, Charlotte was tugging at his belt. "Shit, Char, you're in a hurry." Then he pulled her down into a prone position while Charlotte was eager and wasn't in the mood to wait any longer.

"I want you now," she said huskily.

"Help yourself," he replied while she pulled his jeans off. Their passion took over, and nothing else mattered.

A short time later, they lay side by side. The only sound was the chirping of crickets and the mooing of cows in the distance.

The legion was marching in a column along the center of a shallow valley dotted with oak trees and dense pine groves. Lucius marched at the head of the three cohorts. In the van was Cohort Mars, followed by Jupiter and Apollo.

Plutonius's scouts were far ahead. The sound of the marching men was a constant rumble of footsteps, jangling equipment, and murmured voices. There was no way to keep the noise down.

Charlotte lay naked beside Stefan with her head resting on his chest. Her heart was racing. Stefan gazed up at the night sky and idly played with Charlotte's hair.

She lifted her head to kiss him. He knew she wanted more. But suddenly, she stiffened and glanced around, her hair slapping his face.

"What is it?" he asked.

"Do you hear that?"

"Hear what?" Then he noticed a strange thrumming sound down the valley to the west.

"Somebody's coming!"

Stefan had no intention of being caught naked with an underage girl. "Get dressed!" They pulled on their clothes as the sound resolved itself into an uneven tromping. They ran for the BMW. Climbing on, he hit the starter button. Once Charlotte was behind him, he turned the bike around and drove along the edge of the grove. Just before he reached the road, he stopped.

"What are you doing?" she asked in a frightened whisper.

"Be quiet," he hissed. "I'm trying to figure out where it's coming from. We don't want to run right into it." Then he saw movement to the left. Out in the open, close to where they'd lain only three minutes before, a man walked alone. Stefan couldn't make out any detail in the starlight. The man was wearing some sort of helmet and carried a spear or pole. "What the hell is that," he whispered.

"I can't see," Charlotte said behind him.

Then three more men appeared behind the first one. They wore dark blankets over their shoulders that didn't conceal the dull glint of armor. Their legs were bare.

Stefan started to say something but stopped when hundreds of men came into view. They were marching in a long column. It looked like something from the Euro History Channel. It was an army of armored soldiers carrying spears. Some held large red shields bearing a winged emblem. The sound of their marching feet and clinking armor drowned out the putter of the idling BMW. The column passed a hundred meters from where Stefan and Charlotte were hiding. It took several minutes before the last men passed by and disappeared up the narrow valley to the east.

"I think that's all," he said in a low voice. "I can't wait to tell Jules about this."

Charlotte gasped. "You can't! If anyone found out we were here, it would get back to my father. Everyone in town knows me."

She was right, but Stefan wasn't about to keep his mouth shut. This was too big, whatever it was. "Shit, I don't have to say you were here."

Her fingers clutched his shoulder. "So what were you doing out here all alone? I mean it. I'll never sleep with you again if you say a word to anyone."

"Okay, okay. I can't have your father finding out about us." He looked to where the men had passed from sight. "I wonder what that was?"

"I don't know, and I don't care." Her tone was urgent. "Let's go."

"Okay," he agreed, steering the motorcycle onto the road. But his mind was on what he'd seen. It had been an army of men marching to battle.

"It is exhilarating to be outside after the long Somnum," said Lucius as they left the small valley behind. He looked at the night sky. It was brilliant with stars. "Septimus said he thinks it must be late summer, probably in Augustus. It is fitting our quest begins in the very time of year named for our great leader."

Marcus nodded. "He is probably long dead, but his legacy lives on. I feel very exposed."

The legatus looked at his friend. "Stealth does not come naturally to us."

"The men are eager to fight."

"Especially Vitellus," Lucius said. "He would charge the Gods of Hell to avenge his father's murder."

"Yes, he would. So would I."

Then Lucius changed the subject. "We must find cover soon." He glanced back at Ursa Major, now behind his shoulder to the west. "It will be dawn in a few hours."

Marcus waved for one of Plutonius's scouts. The man rushed over to him.

"Tell the men in the lead to head into the nearest forest with sufficient cover."

With luck and the help of the gods, the legion would find a place to wait out the day. But if no place was found, they might have to fight. He almost hoped they'd encounter some Gauls. His men needed to feel like soldiers again. It might even satisfy Atticus.

CHAPTER IV

WARRIORS

The attack was swift and savage. The packed ranks of Romans slammed into the hoard of barbarians who began to buckle under the determined and organized onslaught. The barbarians wore simple cloth tunics and leather pants but little armor. Their heavy swords were clumsy at close quarters and did little to slow the armored and disciplined Romans.

A centurion shouted orders in Latin while his men moved relentlessly forward and used their heavy shields to force their way into the rapidly disintegrating enemy. Barbarian yells intermingled with the sound of orders and the clang of steel against wood.

The barbarians broke as small knots of men fell back and ran while the remainder fought for survival. One by one, they fell to the ground and lay still. At last, the victorious Roman legionaries stood in complete control of the battlefield. The field was littered with bodies under the bright summer sun.

The gleaming armor and red tunics of the few Roman dead were bright against the verdant green grass. Slain Romans were gathered in litters and carried back to the rear. A legionary blew a long, curved trumpet. Its blaring notes sounded across the battlefield.

Then the dead barbarians sat up, brushing off dirt and grass. One man was assisted by a legionary who handed him his sword with a smile.

"That was incredible," Braden said as the crowd around him cheered and applauded.

Ann smiled. "Wasn't it? I thought you'd enjoy this."

He hugged her over the wooden arm of the folding chair and planted a kiss on her cheek. "I sure did. Thank you for thinking of it."

They were among over a thousand spectators behind a yellow rope barrier separating them from the battlefield. Braden was dressed in a T-shirt and shorts beneath a NATO ball cap while Ann wore Abercrombie & Fitch summer tans and a wide-brimmed Yves Saint Laurent hat.

After spending Friday night in a quaint bed-and-breakfast outside Mons, they had driven south to a private estate where the owner hosted various military encampments and renaissance fairs.

Braden looked at the brochure in his hand. "The land is regularly rented for living history events. I can't believe we're only a hundred klicks from Brussels," he said. "A world away in time."

"I found it on the Internet. So you can come and watch World War One and Two battles, Waterloo, Agincourt, you name it."

Braden was still reading. "God, they've had Spartans and Persians too. That would be something to see."

Ann rolled her eyes but smiled indulgently.

Today the attraction was a series of living history encampments and battles between barbarian and Roman units from all over Europe. A dozen different standards and banners fluttered their scarlet fingers in the warm breeze over the encampment beyond the battlefield.

After the soldiers policed the field for anything that might harm a child, they dropped the barriers. Braden and Ann joined the spectators touring the camps.

The various units offered talks on the life of the Roman legionary.

The couple walked along the neat rows of tents, noting the functional living conditions. One tent was set up for eight men with all their cooking and personal gear on display. "This is a contubernium," Braden said, pointing out the tent. "These eight men eat, march, work, fight, and sleep together. I've read many books on the Roman Army. So this is a great opportunity to see the real thing, sort of."

Ann was interested and asked questions about the equipment and food.

When a legionary showed her his sword, Braden leaned over and whispered into her ear, "Ask him what the scabbard is called."

She did so, and the soldier flashed a wide white-toothed grin. "It's a wageena, Miss."

"Wageena?" Ann repeated, puzzled.

Braden grinned too. "Spelled V-A-G-I-N-A."

"You're joking!" Ann laughed.

"Nope," he said with a grin. "That's the Latin word for a sheath."

Ann rolled her eyes. "Men and their infantile humor. You were just waiting to spring that one on me, weren't you?"

Braden pretended not to hear as he checked his watch. "At noon, the Romans are scheduled to give a demonstration of battle tactics and weapons. I really want to see that. Let's get something to eat at that sandwich vendor and go back to our seats."

Fifteen minutes later, they were again seated in their lawn chairs and watched the legionaries marching out in full armor. The hot summer sun was directly overhead in the cloudless sky.

"How can they stand being in all that armor in the sun?" Ann asked, adjusting her hat.

Braden shrugged. "I wonder the same thing, but I guess they get used to it. The tunics are wool. Sweat cools down under it, so it's probably tolerable."

"Couldn't make me do it for a million pounds," she grunted, taking a long drink of ice water from a bottle.

A narration over the public address system explained the demonstration, but it was hard to hear over the noise of the spectators. The Romans formed into three centuries with ten ranks of eight men each.

"Why aren't there a hundred men in a century?" she asked.

"Centuries were organized on the breakdown of a cohort of 480 men," Braden explained, pulling a thick beef sandwich from a paper bag. After taking a bite and swallowing, he said, "Each century also had about twenty non-combatants that handled the baggage and supplies. Six centuries formed a cohort. Ten cohorts made a legion." He licked mayonnaise from his fingers.

The Romans lifted their shields over their heads, linking them like overlapping red scales. The men on the flanks shifted their shields to cover their open sides. Braden leaned closer to Ann. "That's called the Testudo, or tortoise. It protects them from spears, arrows, and stones."

Ann was impressed. "Wow, that's bloody incredible. I think I saw some riot police in Belfast doing that on the telly."

"Most modern riot police use tactics from the Roman Army," he explained. "Their shields are nearly the same shape and size, and the helmets differ only in material from the Roman design."

"Amazing," Ann said, her respect for the ancient army increasing.

Next was a demonstration of the pilum. The long harpoon-like spears, Braden told her, were considered the best throwing weapons ever designed.

The Romans threw the long weapons at rows of wooden figures painted to represent a generic barbarian army. Even at the distance of thirty paces, most hit their targets. Then the heavy-handled wood sagged from their weight and bent the metal shaft. "They were designed that way," Braden said when Ann looked at him questioningly. "There were two pins holding the shaft to the handle. One was wood and the other metal. The wood pin broke on impact, making the pila useless. If it hit a shield, the barbs held and the shield was unusable. And spears in the ground impeded the enemy."

Ann watched with rapt attention as the Romans then drew their swords and advanced. "Why are the swords so short?"

"The Gladius España, or Spanish sword, was used for stabbing instead of slashing. A long, heavy sword is fine when you're on a horse or fighting an unarmored foe, but it's no good against armor. Swinging a sword uses a lot of energy. A slash is difficult to aim and rarely fatal. A stab, on the other hand, is more accurate and easier. You can put the point into the gut, under the armor, or in the armpit. It's almost always fatal." He popped the last bite of the sandwich into his mouth.

Braden could be pedantic, but Ann indulged him. "Nasty," she said. "These blokes were the best, weren't they?" She had done well in college history, but this was all new to her.

"Yes," Braden replied. "The Imperial Roman Army was the best professional fighting force that ever existed." He leaned closer to her. "Think about it. With thirty legions, Rome ruled from Africa to Scotland and from Spain to Palestine for close to a thousand years. No other army or civilization ever matched that. I'm fascinated by them."

"I see that," she said with a smile.

The reenactors marched past with their swords poking out from the wall of shields like steel porcupine quills. "They look bloody unstoppable," she observed.

"Yeah," Braden said. "The Romans were unbeatable in battle but only if they fought on ground of their choosing."

She frowned. "I don't understand."

Before he could reply, the barbarians came onto the field and faced their enemy with their weapons. Unlike the legionaries, they were in loose groups and waved their swords and yelled like furies.

The Romans moved forward, never breaking rank or step.

"By the time of Augustus at the beginning of the first century, they'd become pretty confident. Even cocky, I guess you could say."

"In what way?"

Braden watched the two armies approach one another before answering. "Well, the Empire had pacified the inhabitants over nearly all of Europe. They thought they were invincible."

"Weren't they?" Ann asked. "Look at them," she said, pointing at the men on the field. "Who had any chance against that lot?"

Braden smiled. "The Roman Army did suffer defeats. In AD 7, Augustus ordered a former Governor of Africa and Syria named Quinctilius Varus to assemble five legions in northern France. Varus wasn't a professional soldier but a lawyer. I think he was a senator and married to Augustus's grand-niece. Roman nepotism."

Ann grinned. "Still a lot of that going on."

"Yes," Braden said. "Varus led three legions into a region of northeastern Germany in the spring of AD 9."

"Two thousand years ago?"

"Yep. The Seventeenth, Eighteenth, and Nineteenth legions patrolled the region and maintained order while Varus conducted a census and imposed taxes on the population. There were a lot of protests. Varus was brutal in how he put them down. That caused a lot of resentment toward the Romans in Germania. A German prince named Arminius told Varus about an uprising of German tribes west of the Weser River. Arminius had been a respected auxiliary officer in the army for years. But he was plotting to bring down Rome's rule in Germania once and for all."

"Arminius?" Ann asked. "That sounds like a Latin name."

"His Germanic name was Armann, which became Hermann."

"Interesting. What happened?"

"The three legions numbered close to fifteen thousand troops. They also had about half that number of camp followers and families. The entire column must have been miles long."

"Blimey," Ann said as she looked out at the demonstration, but her attention was on Braden's narrative.

"Varus entered a huge wooded region named the Teutoberg Forest near modern-day Osnabrück. There's a hill called Kalkriese. Some of the German Auxiliaries marching with the column slipped away and disappeared into the forest. Varus didn't see any reason for concern."

"Well, he had fifteen thousand men."

"But they were in a confined area with swamp on one side and a ridge covered in thick trees on the other. A bad place for a battle." He paused, watching the field. His timing was perfect. "And then it happened."

At that instant, the barbarians charged at a full run at the Romans. A moment later, they smashed themselves against their enemy with the resounding rumble of wood against steel. The audience cheered, and Braden waited until it subsided. "Arminius had arranged a well-organized ambush. They loosed thousands of arrows from the hillsides and then attacked both flanks of the column. The Romans had no chance to set up a defense and were cut down by arrows, spears, and human wave attacks. The battle lasted for three days. The Germans were ruthless. They killed and butchered thousands upon thousands, including the civilians."

Ann's face paled under her hat. With the scene on the field before her, she had little difficulty imagining the ancient horror he was recounting. "How many survived?"

Braden's voice was somber. "Out of twenty-five thousand, only a few hundred escaped."

Her eyes widened. "Is that all?"

He merely nodded.

"They couldn't fight back?"

He shook his head. "Look out there. They're winning because they have room to maneuver. All Arminius needed to do was get them into an area where they couldn't fight back effectively."

"Varus trusted him?"

"Yep. I'm sure there were many officers who didn't think walking into that forest was a good idea, but Varus must have ignored them."

"Was he killed?"

"He killed himself rather than be tortured by the Germans. The battle is called the Varian Disaster, sometimes the Teutoberg Massacre."

"Rather like Ishandlwana in 1879," Ann said. "The Zulus killed an entire regiment of British troops."

Braden nodded. "And Custer's Last Stand, but on a much larger scale."

On the field, the barbarians were being pushed back by the Roman advance. Then the trumpets sounded, and it was over.

"What happened afterward?" Ann wanted to know.

"Augustus took it hard," Braden said. "He used to walk around the palace and beat the walls saying, 'Quinctilius Varus, give me back my legions!' In fact, after the battle, there was never again a seventeenth, eighteenth, or nineteenth legion in the Roman Army. Their banners were retired."

Ann inquired if the Romans had ever gone back into Germany.

"Yes and no." Braden pulled a bottle of beer from a cooler pack. He looked at the label with a wry smile. It was a German lager. He used his Swiss Army knife to pop the cap and took a pull before answering. "Augustus recommended to the Senate that they shouldn't expand the Empire. He said they had more than enough to deal with. So the Roman garrisons in Gaul built several more forts along the Rhine River."

"But somebody had to have gone back into Germany," Ann persisted.

He took another drink. "About six years after the battle, a legion led by Germanicus found the site. They found the roads and forest littered with dismembered skeletons. The Germans had made it into a slaughterhouse by hacking the bodies to pieces, impaling heads onto trees with spears, all sorts of horrible things. It was a clear message: 'Don't fuck with us.'"

Ann shook her head. "How awful."

"It was just as catastrophic to the Romans as Pearl Harbor was to the United States." He took off his cap and ran the cool bottle over his forehead. "For almost two thousand years, the site of the massacre was lost to history. Finally it was discovered in the 1980s by some archaeologists who uncovered some Roman coins. No coins were minted after AD 9, so they had to have been from Varus's column. Later, more artifacts were found. It's an archaeological site now."

The demonstration was over, and they stood to gather their things. Ann was silent, but Braden sensed that she was thinking about what he'd told her. Finally, she turned to him. "It was a lot different in those days, I suppose. A lot more savage."

He gave her an ironic smile. "In some ways, I guess. But mankind has managed to do a lot worse in the last century. Remember the Holocaust?"

"I know what you're saying, and I agree. But I'd hate to think of what would happen if the Romans were still around today. Like you said, they conquered most of the western world back then."

"Yes. They would be a lot more dangerous now."

Braden's car was a white 2018 Peugeot he'd leased for his tour with NATO. He pulled open the driver's door and climbed in, reaching over the tan leather upholstery to unlock Ann's door. She got in, and they followed the line of departing cars to the main road. "Where to next, Ann?"

"Follow the road until you get to the highway and turn south."

"Right-O." He turned on the stereo. The CD player poured forth George Winston. Ann closed her eyes while the deep notes of "Variations on the Kanon" filled the Peugeot's interior. He turned onto the main highway as "Cast Your Fate into the Wind" came on. Before long, the rolling grassy hills of central Belgium gave way to the thick trees and clustered ridges of the Ardennes Forest. Ann pointed to a turnoff toward Liège. After they had passed through the ancient city, she directed him up a winding road where they reached a tall stone and iron gate. Braden's eyes widened. In front of the car's white hood was a splendid old hotel. It was very nearly a castle with stone walls, tall towers, and leaded diamond-paned windows. He pulled into a space under the shade of a tree alongside Volvos and Mercedes sedans.

Ann got out and went to check in while he retrieved their bags. When he entered the lobby, he gaped in awe. A huge copper chandelier hung from the beamed ceiling. The floor was solid stone, like something from *A Connecticut Yankee in King Arthur's Court*. While Ann filled out the paperwork, he admired the elegant red velvet upholstered furniture.

A long sweeping stone staircase wound up to the second-floor balcony. The concierge, an older man with a ring of white hair circling his head, led them upstairs to a long corridor interspersed with heavy oak doors and medieval furnishings. Iron lamp sconces and tapestries hung from the walls. Stopping at a door, he unlocked it with a key and swung it open.

After following Ann inside, Braden dropped the bags by the door and took a look around the room. A thick carpet covered the oak floor. Opposite the entrance, heavy dark-green damask draperies framed twin Gothic windows. The golden afternoon sun cast long bars of light onto a four-poster canopied bed. The man handed him the key. "I hope your stay here will be pleasant," he said sincerely. "If you need or want anything at all, please call me. My name is Rudolpho. The front desk number is 00." He bowed and left the room.

"Well, did I do good?" Ann asked.

Braden nodded dumbly. "I'll say you did." Only Ann's considerable travel agent discount could make a palace like this affordable. He walked around the room. A stone fireplace dominated one end. Above the mantel was a shield emblazoned with a coat of arms featuring a lion and an eagle. "All it needs is a badger and snake," he said with a grin.

Ann didn't get it at first, then laughed. "Oh yes. It does remind me of Hogwarts. Do you like it?"

"It's fantastic. Like a trip back in time." Looking out a window, he saw an elegant garden, a large hedge maze, and an ornate fish pond with a fountain. "No tennis courts," he said approvingly. He went over to Ann and hugged her. "You're truly amazing, honey."

"Supper will be served in an hour," she said. "Want to take a bath first?" She walked into a door set to the left of the bed, shedding Abercrombie & Fitch as she went.

Braden was no fool. He followed her into the bathroom. Again his eyes widened. A long, tiled counter set with two marble sinks and gold fixtures was under a gilt-framed mirror. He saw the reflection of what was behind him. Made of gleaming black marble, the bathtub was over seven feet long and shaped like a cloverleaf. "Now that's a bathtub," he exclaimed. It looked incredibly erotic, made more so by the sight of Ann, now nude and bending over to turn on the water from another gold faucet. "Well, love, let's get a move on. I don't want to be late for supper."

Braden didn't need another invitation. Her full breasts hung invitingly over the foaming water. As great as it had been so far, the weekend was only going to get better.

CHAPTER V

THE NEW WORLD

Plutonius's scouts had found a deep valley with thick trees as the golden sun peaked over a ridge to the east. The legionaries dug shallow pits in the dark soft soil and settled in for the day, covering themselves with blankets and branches. They drank water and munched on the grapes they'd brought from the cellar. The warm sun crept across the sky. It was the first daylight they had seen in a long time, and few of the legionaries felt like sleeping.

Lucius was wide awake, excited at being out and again on the march. But by the time the sun reached its zenith, he had fallen asleep.

It seemed as if he'd just closed his eyes when he felt a hand shaking his shoulder. "Sire, it is time to wake," he heard Septimus saying in a whisper. "The sun is down."

Lucius grunted and raised his head. After rubbing his face, he looked around him to see his men standing and gathering their gear. "Very well, Septimus," he said. "Assemble the men for the march. The same orders apply."

"Already being done," said Marcus. "I awoke at dusk."

Lucius didn't bother scolding them for not waking him. He had been tired. "Good. As soon as we are ready, have Plutonius lead off." Just then, the medicus approached him and saluted. "Sire, may I have a word with you?"

Sensing the man did not want to be overheard, Lucius gestured for the orderly to follow him away from the legionaries around him. He thought he knew what it was about. "What is it?"

"I found three more dead men, Sire. They died in their sleep, just as the ones in the cellar. They were all from Cohort Apollo."

Lucius nodded. "I understand. Just watch the rest and keep me informed." He paused. "How many medicii are there besides you?"

"Three, Sire."

"I realize you will be caring for a thousand men, but do your best. Have the dead men buried. We do not have time to find out what killed them." Seeing Marcus and Septimus listening, Lucius waved them over. "Tell Vitellus and Atticus to keep watch on their men," he said. "When a legionary dies on the march, bury him at once. Do not wait for orders."

"Yes, Sire," was the dual reply.

"I am sure this will only give Atticus more fuel for his fire," muttered Marcus.

"What do you mean?" Lucius looked at the big man next to him. He realized this was something Marcus had been waiting to say.

"I know he is a good soldier and has never been seen to waver in his duty, but he does not seem to be as . . . ah, dedicated to our cause as Vitellus."

There was more. "Go on," Lucius pressed.

"Vitellus told me he heard Atticus talking to Sestus of his anger that we had lost so many men. He is saying that we should return to Rome. The German traitors are surely long dead, and there can be no justice."

Lucius felt his skin run cold. "What about Sestus?"

"Sestus was reluctant to agree with Atticus."

Lucius mulled this over. "He is young and eager. Both of his uncles died in Germania. He is loyal to our cause, but Atticus may poison some of his men. We have lost so many. I do not want an entire cohort to desert us. Atticus was not in Germania."

"No. Vitellus told me Atticus joined because he would be given cohort command."

"Yes, I remember. But his service record was flawless." He leaned close to Marcus. "I want to know anything else Atticus says along these lines."

Marcus nodded. "Vitellus wants to cut his heart out, but it is not his place to do so."

It would be mine, Lucius thought, wondering if it might ultimately be necessary to execute Atticus. "That remains to be seen. For now, let us move on."

When the grove they had taken shelter in gave way to open pasture, Lucius remarked, "I remember this region to be endless dense forest. Where have all the trees gone?"

Marcus nodded. "Cut down for construction or firewood. But to eradicate entire forests would take many generations."

"But how many? That is what I want to know."

Their line of march took them through a series of shallow valleys between low ridges. They tried to avoid open areas and skirted around the boundaries of the many farms. It seemed that every mile they covered was divided by fences, stone walls, or hedges. These had to be surmounted or bypassed, which slowed their advance. "These people must fortify everything they own," Marcus said as they worked their way through yet another thick hedgerow. "It is like a maze."

Lucius agreed, watching as his men threaded through a narrow opening. He heard the barking of a large dog in the distance. "They all seem to have dogs. They bark at everything."

The night had a thousand eyes. Lucius could not believe how hellishly stressful it was to be exposed in the night. Stealth and caution were alien to the Roman Army. At any moment they might be seen by a person looking out a window at the wrong moment. Someone going past in one of the metal chariots or even a person taking a stroll in the dark could see them and raise the alarm. It was only by the blessing of the gods that it had not happened. But Lucius knew their good fortune could not last.

When they reached a road, they crossed quickly in small groups while scouts watched for the metal chariots. Fortunately, all the chariots had bright lamps that were easy to see from a great distance. They saw the lights of small groups of houses and what appeared to be places of meeting where many chariots gathered. Overhead the sky had become a deep blue-black; it looked brighter than Lucius remembered from the days before the Somnum. He was about to comment but was interrupted when Septimus ran up to him.

"Sire," Septimus said in an unusually strident voice. "Look at that!"

Lucius looked up where Septimus was pointing. There, among the millions of stars, one was moving very fast. He glared at his friend. "It is a falling star," he said dismissively.

"No," insisted Septimus. "Please look again."

Lucius did. Then his eyes widened. The star was blinking very regularly, like a drum beat. He stopped walking. It was not falling like a meteor but moving across the sky in a straight line.

He heard voices murmuring behind him. "What in the name of Apollo is it?" he asked. "A winged chariot?"

"I do not know," Septimus said, clearly awed at the sight.

Lucius watched the strange object until it disappeared to the north. He signaled for the march to resume. But he could not resist looking up, still wondering what they had seen.

They marched on, passing through small groves and crossing over streams. They heard the bleating and mooing of livestock in the distance.

Marcus grunted. "Those cows are making my stomach rumble. We need fresh meat."

"Yes," his leader agreed. "Have some details forage as we march to find whatever they can."

Marcus gave the order to Vitellus in Cohort Jupiter, then resumed walking beside Lucius. "A goblet of Posca would be nice," he said.

Lucius smiled to himself. He had been thinking nearly the same thing. "Yes, or even Ascetum," he said with a grin. "We drank that in Germania."

The giant spat. "I am not that desperate. Let the barbarians drink poison. Posca wine would do me fine."

Foraging on the march was second nature to the Roman Army, and soon the men had gathered bushels of apples, nuts, and grapes. Two sheep were also taken from a farm. Once they had been quietly killed, they were carried on the backs of two strong men.

"Marcus," Lucius said, "we have to see what lies ahead."

The dark giant indicated a high tree-lined hill to their left. "Up there. That may be high enough."

Lucius ordered Septimus to rest the men while he and Marcus climbed the hill. Bathed in sweat and breathing hard, they reached the crest and looked out at the vast panorama beyond.

"Oh, great Caesar," Marcus said in a throaty whisper.

Spread out in an immense vista that stretched to the horizon was a world of wonder. They'd become used to seeing the lights of farms and houses, but what they saw now went far beyond their experience. In the distance were small towns connected by roads winding in and out of the hills. They intersected one another in a bewildering maze of lines and angles. Lucius saw tiny lights moving along them. *By the gods, there are so many*, he thought, shivering in the cool breeze on the hilltop. *So few of us. And we are growing fewer.* His ruminations were interrupted by Marcus.

"Sirius is far to the west. It is well past midnight. It appears this new world does not sleep."

Lucius said nothing. He was still thinking about what they faced. Turning to the south, he saw a large town illuminated in a solid glowing grid of white and yellow. "It is as though the stars have fallen onto the Earth. Did you ever imagine such a sight as this, Marcus?"

The big man shook his head. "Never in my life, Lucius Cassius."

To the east, ranks of ridges bent toward a meandering river. Lucius saw humped black shapes of forested hills beyond the far bank. There were few lights over that way. Pointing to the river, Lucius said, "We will cross that river. But how do we reach it without being seen?"

The tall man did something he'd never had to do at night in his entire life. He shielded his eyes from the glare. "Down that way is a dark region we might use. I see no lights."

Lucius saw the place he indicated. "Good. We will make camp on this side of the river and cross tomorrow night. Let us go."

They took one last look at the incredible sight, then moved down the hill to where the legion waited. Marcus told Plutonius where to go.

On the march again, Lucius told Septimus what they'd seen. The scholarly officer wanted to know more, but it would keep until they had reached cover.

Turning to Marcus, Lucius said, "The river we saw, do you know which one it is?"

"It is the Meuse," Marcus replied, taking off his helmet to wipe the sweat from his brow.

For a long moment Lucius absorbed the words. His mind immediately went back to when he first arrived in Gallicae to begin his training. Legio XVIII had been encamped in a fort along the bank of the Meuse River. There he had undergone four grueling months of the hardest work and training he could ever have imagined. In a way, it had been the first step in the long odyssey that brought him to this very place. "The Meuse," he murmured. "I wonder if the fort still exists." He looked into the darkness to the south.

"The river is not very wide this time of year," Marcus said. "There is a great forest in the hills beyond."

"In Belgicae," Lucius said, remembering. "And beyond that is the Rhenus River." Then his dark eyes almost blazed with renewed vigor.

Marcus knew what his leader was thinking. "In Germania Superior. Our goal."

Feeling as if they had finally gained some idea of what to do next, Lucius craned his head around to look for Sirius. The star was almost out of sight behind them. "Tell the men to quicken their pace."

Two hours later, as the stars faded in the purple predawn light, they rounded a hill and saw an area of woods stretching down to the river.

"Move into the trees," Lucius ordered his officers. "Find cover and then the men can eat. But these woods are not thick enough to permit cooking fires. Roasting the mutton will have to wait." The other faces betrayed their disappointment but they understood their orders.

At the edge of the woods, they stopped. On the ground, a curious double line of thick metal bars extended into the distance in either direction. They were spiked onto hundreds of heavy wooden beams.

What in the world could these be? Lucius wondered silently. Bending down to touch the cold metal, he said, "It is incredible that a civilization can use metal so lavishly. The metal in these bars would armor an entire army."

Marcus was smiling. "This is proof Rome does rule this region. Who else could have conceived such a road as this?"

Lucius was not so sure, but there were more important things on his mind. He stood and saw the last men of Cohort Apollo moving into the dark woods. Tall elms and oaks blotted out the lightening sky. The ground was thick with brush and dead leaves, providing comfortable resting places. Plutonius and his men scouted down to the riverbank and reported they saw no roads or houses, only a few animal trails. The cohorts arranged themselves in tight rings about thirty paces in size, each man facing outward toward any threat. In every pair of men, one slept while the other kept watch with his weapons ready. Lucius pulled off his helmet and turned to Plutonius. "Place some sentries around our camp and relieve them at mid-day."

Septimus stood beside him. "What should we do if someone does blunder into our camp?"

The question was greeted with a raised eyebrow.

Marcus grinned in amusement. "Invite them into camp to share our meal, Septimus Deo." The three men laughed while they settled in for the long wait.

Lucius munched on an apple. "I hope we can cook the sheep soon." He looked toward Cohort Apollo and saw Atticus talking with Sestus. *I wonder what they are saying.* Sestus was new to command. He was eager to prove himself. Then Lucius saw the olive-skinned Atticus point toward him. Sestus turned and for a moment his pale eyes met those of his legatus. Lucius made sure the younger man saw him looking back at him. Then Sestus saluted Atticus, turning away and sitting down out of Lucius's sight.

Just as sleep began to close over him, Lucius felt a trembling in the ground. As a boy, he'd been through a mild earthquake, and it had produced nearly the same sensation. Then he heard a rumbling sound like an approaching avalanche. He sat up and saw the men near him snapping their heads around, hefting their weapons while searching for the source of the noise. It seemed to be coming from where they'd entered the trees.

Suddenly a loud, dissonant howl like a huge hunting dog cut through the late-morning air. Every legionary stood, alert and ready.

A moment later the howl ended, leaving a dead hole in the air. Then the pitch of the rumble changed and turned into a rhythmic clatter like the sound of gears in a water mill. A sentry ran up to Lucius. His eyes were wide.

"Sire, I saw it!"

"What was it?" Lucius asked, drawing his gladius.

"It was huge, like a building and very long. I could not see the end of it." Spreading his arms, he tried to convey an object of immense size and strength. "The head was a titanic metal vessel, bigger than a war galley. It moved faster than a horse could run. Behind the head were many more, each one the size of a building."

"But there are no roads nearby," Marcus commented.

Turning to the other officer, the legionary said, "It traveled on the metal bands we found outside the wood."

Marcus and Lucius exchanged glances. "Tell me more," Lucius prompted.

"I never saw the tail of it. All the while I was running here, I heard it still moving past."

Lucius tried to imagine what the man was describing. He nodded. "Good report, legionary. Return to your post."

But the man did not leave. Lucius noted his hesitation. "Yes?"

"Sire, there is one more thing." He looked down at the ground before speaking. He was obviously dreading what he was about to say. "There were people looking out of windows. Many of them."

Lucius glanced at Marcus with a frown. "Did any of them see you?"

The legionary said nothing for a moment, then said, "Yes, Sire. I was well into the trees but they saw me. Some of them were shouting and waving at me."

For a long moment Lucius and Marcus remained silent. Then the legatus nodded. "Do not concern yourself. You did your duty. Resume your post. You will be relieved at mid-day."

As the man walked away, Lucius said, "All we can do is hope nothing comes of it."

But he knew better.

CHAPTER VI

CROSSINGS

"Did you enjoy the weekend?" Ann asked Braden on the drive back to Brussels. It was Sunday afternoon and the sky was turning a rosy shade of pale blue.

"I sure did," he replied, savoring some of the memories. After rising at the comfortable hour of ten o'clock, they'd ordered breakfast from the excellent hotel kitchen and dined at a table set on the lushly planted back patio. After eating, they had decided to explore the hedge maze.

"How do we get out?" Ann asked once they entered the twisting labyrinth of three-meter-tall hedges.

"Oh, we'll find it," Braden said with exaggerated confidence. "Don't worry."

Ann wasn't so sure. The maze covered over three thousand square meters. She gamely pressed on, working her way into the bewildering turns. She didn't notice that Braden was leisurely following at a distance, his left hand gently brushing the greenery as he walked.

After nearly half an hour, they emerged at the maze's central courtyard. It was furnished with marble benches arranged around a small pond stocked with colorful fish and lily pads.

Another couple was sitting on a bench. They greeted Braden and Ann with polite smiles.

"Looks to me like they're as lost as we are," Ann observed.

"Relax, honey. Let's enjoy the experience." He noted which of the four openings in the hedge they'd exited and sat down. The other couple was a German dentist and his newly pregnant schoolteacher wife. They chatted with one another about the local attractions until Ann suggested they try and find their way out. Both couples left the quiet atrium, each heading for a different opening.

This time Braden led the way and, without hesitation, started into the labyrinth. Ann simply followed, wondering if they'd have to yell for help.

But Braden kept moving and never took a wrong turn. Ann could only watch in incredulity as they exited the maze less than ten minutes after starting out.

"How in the bloody hell did you know the way to go? We must have taken a dozen wrong turns when we went in."

Braden shrugged. "I have a good sense of direction. Should we go and see the town?"

She stood at the maze entrance with a scowl. "You found a map and crammed, didn't you?"

"A map? What map?" His innocent look failed to mollify her. Finally Braden relented. "Okay, I give. Did you notice I stayed back and let my left hand follow the left wall?"

"You left a trail!"

"No, of course not. I've been to Hampton Court. That maze is intricate, but there is a trick to it."

Ann waited.

"When you enter, keep one hand on the wall and don't take any course or turn that forces you to remove that hand. Eventually you'll reach the inside. When you head out, put your other hand on the same wall and do the same thing. If you don't remove your hand, you'll reach the same exit. It's an ironclad rule of topology."

She frowned and turned back toward the maze. The German couple hadn't yet come out. She began to laugh. "Where in the hell did you pick up that little trick?"

"Oh, something I picked up in an old *Time-Life* book on mathematics when I was a kid." He cocked an eyebrow. "You know me, Ann. I can't resist figuring out a puzzle. I have to know the answer no matter what."

They walked back toward the hotel. Ann heard a man's voice calling out in German.

"Hello? Can someone help us find our way out?"

They shared a quiet laugh as Rudolpho walked past them and headed to the maze.

The smile remained on Braden's face, but he was already thinking ahead to Monday. Scudding clouds darkened the eastern sky as the spires and buildings of Brussels came into view ahead. "Looks like we got lucky on the weather. I think it'll rain tonight," he said.

"Lucky?" Ann said with an indignant look. "I arranged that too. I have connections."

With a laugh Braden said, "I don't doubt it." He turned into the entrance drive at the hotel she used when in Belgium. Leaving the Peugeot running, he retrieved her bags and handed them to the doorman. "Thanks for a wonderful trip back in time, honey."

"Glad you enjoyed it." She gave him a curious smile. "I'm surprised how fascinating I found the reenactment. It's not my usual cup of tea. But you made it more fun. That's one of the reasons I love you."

He returned her smile. "I thought it was my good looks and charming wit."

She cocked her head as if thinking hard. "You have a charming wit?" She kissed him and waved as he climbed into the car. He drove away, already thinking about the next day's work.

When the sun had disappeared behind the hills to the west, the legion began preparing for the night's march. First they had to get across the river. Lucius and Marcus were in conference with Arcturius, the engineer. "Sire," Arcturius began, "we found a good place to ford the river." He pointed at a coil of thick rope piled next to his armor. "Each of my engineers has plenty of rope. With those tied to trees on the banks, the men can pull themselves along."

"How deep is the river?" Marcus asked.

Arcturius, who was of average height, revealed his tunic under the blanket. It was wet up to his waist. "This is the deepest I found. The bottom is mud with some rocks. I think it is late summer. The river is not very deep. I used a pilum to give myself support."

Lucius gave him a nod. "Very well. Get started."

He felt pride and disquiet. During the day, six legionaries had died. Lucius ordered them buried under the trees.

They reached the riverbank. The Meuse River was a wide black expanse of moving water. It curved away into the darkness. It was not moving swiftly, but the rippled surface was in constant motion. Arcturius indicated where they would cross. "It is about a hundred paces to the other bank," he said, pointing at a spot on the far side. "My four strongest men will take two ropes across and tie them to those trees. I believe about twenty men at a time can hold the ropes and pull themselves across."

"Very good," Lucius said. "Do it."

Each carrying a pilum and rope that had been tied to a tree on the near bank, the four men made their way across the slowly moving black water. In a short time, they had reached the far bank and tied the ropes to a stout tree.

Lucius stepped forward. "I will go first."

"The water is warm, Sire," Arcturius said. "But the current is quite strong. I beg you, hold the ropes tightly."

With Marcus and his officers watching, Lucius took the upstream guide rope and followed it out into the river. The water was warm and quickly swallowed his feet and legs. The bottom mud was not deep, but it sucked at his caligae with every step. Before he reached the center of the river, he felt the relentless tug of the current against his legs and body. He had to hold the rope with both hands to keep from losing his footing. *The men with heavy equipment will have to secure their load in order to hold the rope,* he thought. *If any man falls into the water, he will drown before we can pull him out.* Lucius moved up onto the bank. In the back of his mind, he realized he was almost in Belgicae, one step closer to their goal.

Marcus was at his side a few minutes later. "Easy enough, Lucius Cassius."

"Go back and tell Vitellus and the others that the men will have to tie on their gear. They need both hands to cross."

Marcus grinned and shook the water from his legs. "I did not need to."

Lucius cocked his head. "No river could carry you away, but not all our men are as heavy. Now go."

Plutonius's scouts were the next to cross. "See what lies ahead," Lucius told them.

The crossing was slow, but the legionaries plodded through the water at a steady pace. One enterprising legionary tried using his upturned scutum as a makeshift boat, and he was able to carry his impedimenta across without difficulty. Most of the others copied this and easily made it to the far bank. Some men lost their footing in the relentless current but having their hands free kept them from being swept away. A few men did lose cooking or entrenching tools, but they sank out of sight. Once they were across, they were told to go into the trees and wait. Two hours after Lucius had stepped into the river, the entire legion was across and the ropes retrieved.

"That was an adventure," Marcus said to Lucius.

"The men did well," the legatus said with pride. "We have marched for two nights and have not met any opposition. Soon we will reach Germania." He did not say anything about the sentry being seen by those people. He did not have to. He knew Marcus and the rest of his officers were thinking the same thing. Would the alarm be sounded?

Plutonius stepped up to Lucius. "There is a road a short distance ahead, Sire. It cuts across our route of march."

"Did you see any of the armored vehicles?"

"Yes. More than three score of the chariots passed in both directions. Not a one was like another. Different sizes, shapes, and colors. None had horses or other means to pull it."

Septimus arrived in time to hear this. "They may not be military chariots as we supposed. Perhaps they are made of metal because that is what they use on everything. In our time it was used only when no other material was sufficient. But now it may be very common."

Lucius mulled this over. "You are probably right, but they are still dangerous enough to avoid."

Plutonius continued. "We crested a low ridge on the other side. There are a few farms and small towns to the south. Beyond was solid, dense forest as far as we could see."

"Excellent," Marcus said with a broad grin. "We will be able to cook our meat."

Lucius shook his head in amusement. Marcus was known for his insatiable appetite. "How long will it take us to reach the Rhenus?"

Marcus rubbed his chin. "It is heavy forest down the valley of the Sauer River until it drains into the Moselle. If we stay away from any farms and towns, we should reach the Rhenus in about two or three more nights."

Lucius considered this. "I recall we followed those rivers when we began the Germanic campaign. The region was very sparsely inhabited then. Perhaps we will find it much the same." He did not sound hopeful.

A short time later, they reached the road. It was about twenty paces wide and black-surfaced with a white line painted along the center. It curved through the forest, disappearing into the distance. Lucius was standing when Plutonius hissed sharply, "Sire, get down! A chariot is coming!"

Lucius ducked behind a bush and watched the armored chariot move past. It was about the size of a mill wagon and made of a shiny white metal. It made a droning noise that reminded him of a swarm of angry bees. In a second it had passed in a rush of air and noise. He looked at Marcus. "They move very fast."

The big man nodded and turned to Plutonius. "Station two men a hundred paces in each direction. Tie a strip of cloth to their pila. Wave them from side to side when they see a chariot coming. When it is clear, move it up and down. Do you understand?"

"Yes, Sire," Plutonius said.

When the all-clear signal was seen in both directions, Lucius led the first group across at a run. This went surprisingly fast; they were deep into the dense forest in less than an hour. The skies began to cloud over and the air became cool. The men pulled their blankets closer.

An hour after crossing the road, they came to another one that ran parallel to a metal fence. It was made of a strong wire mesh and had signs along it. No one could read the wording, but the word "Belges" was familiar. "This may be the border between Gallicae and Belgicae," Lucius said. He looked at the fence, which was about as tall as Marcus. "We can climb over this."

Another hour passed as the legionaries surmounted the obstacle and resumed the march into the woods. Fortunately, they saw none of the metal chariots on the road.

The legion eventually entered a clearing that was surrounded by dense forest. Lucius made a decision. He raised his hand. "We will stop here. We have put enough distance between ourselves and the river." He waved for Regulus. "Pick some good hunters and find game. It is safe here to build small fires."

The order was greeted with smiles. Lucius said to Plutonius, "Form a perimeter. Tell the sentries to stay close enough to warn us if they see anything."

By the time three small fire pits had been lit, Regulus's archers returned with a large buck deer suspended from a pole.

"I came upon him at a stream," Centaurus said proudly. "My brother Sirius and I crept close, and I brought him down with a single arrow."

Lucius looked at the large beast. "Well done. I want the meat cooked quickly." He looked at the dark, cloudy sky through the branches overhead and smelled the night air. "It will rain soon."

The deer and sheep were quickly butchered. Cuts of meat were spitted onto the pila over the fires, and soon the rich aroma of roasting meat filled the air. Before long, each cohort gathered at a fire to receive its ration of venison or mutton. A few legionaries joked about the lack of wine and seasonings, but they were glad to have fresh meat for the first time since leaving the cellar.

Marcus licked his fingers after devouring a cut of roast venison. "We can live well in this new world. At least deer tastes the same."

"New world," Septimus repeated while looking at the dark woods around them. "Yes, it is indeed a new world. Chariots without horses, strange moving lights in the sky, huge metal vessels that travel on rails." He shook his head. "How long has it been?"

Lucius finished his meat and drank from his water bag. Then he smiled.

Septimus saw his commander's expression. "What is so amusing, Lucius Cassius?"

"I was thinking," he said, still grinning, "that this is the best meal I've eaten in centuries."

CHAPTER VII

FATAL ENCOUNTER

Sergeant Herbert St. Paul drove the Belgian State Police sedan south along the Boullion Road through the vast Ardennes Forest. Seated next to him was his new partner, Patrolman Henrí Dumont, who was fifteen years younger than the forty-year-old veteran sergeant.

They were driving their regular Sunday night patrol east of the French border. The tall trees and thick underbrush totally obscured everything beyond thirty meters.

It was a quiet night. So far, all they had done was ticket a speeder and call a tow truck for a stranded French motorist. "Not much happens on Sunday night," Dumont said, wondering if he had made the right choice in transferring from the hectic Friday and Saturday evening shifts. At least he met plenty of cute girls. But the pay grade for the Sunday to Monday shift was higher.

St. Paul, who had been on this duty for over two years, knew better. In any case he preferred quiet duty. The only drawback was the night shift supervisor, Kurt Hoster, whose pugnacious and authoritarian personality caused no end of difficulty for the officers and staff. But at least he didn't have to be around him when on the road. "It is often quiet," St. Paul agreed in his laconic manner. "But you never know what might happen."

They crested a rise in the road and were able to see several kilometers in all directions. Then something caught St. Paul's eye. He slowed the car and pulled over. Rising from the thick forest to the west was a thin trail of pale smoke. Beyond it was another and a third. Three fires. He pointed. "Do you see them?"

Dumont looked to the west. He saw the smoke, and beneath it, the subdued orange-green glow of small fires. "Yes, Sergeant. Two—no—three campfires."

"Yes," St. Paul affirmed. "Deep in the woods in the summer. Very dangerous. We'll have to cite them."

He picked up the radio handset. "Bastogne Dispatch, Patrol 37. We're going to investigate some open campfires near the border. Over."

"Understood, Patrol 37," came the dispatcher's voice over the radio. "What is your position? Over."

St. Paul checked the GPS. "Dispatch, Patrol 37. We're on the Boullion Road, grid 11-92. Over."

"Acknowledged. Grid 11-92. Bastogne Dispatch out."

St. Paul hooked a small hand radio on his belt next to the service-issue Walther PP 9mm pistol.

"There's a hiking trail just ahead," St. Paul said. "We'll go in and investigate."

He climbed out of the driver's seat and closed the door.

St. Paul stood almost two meters tall, solidly built, and looked the image of a cop. He wore a light gray police jacket over his uniform.

Dumont exited the car and followed his partner.

St. Paul knew the Ardennes well. He walked with the skill of a practiced woodsman.

Dumont tried to duplicate the sergeant's movements. He was nervous about working with St. Paul, one of the Staatsveiligheid, the Belgian State Security Service's most experienced officers. St. Paul was often assigned new men to teach and guide them. His methods were sometimes unconventional, and Dumont never knew when the older man would do something contrary to the police manual.

Dumont reassured himself by patting the holster of his own pistol.

He had been with the Security Service for only three months. He was shorter than his partner, with blond hair and the beginnings of a mustache on his narrow face.

"It must be hunters or campers," he commented.

"Hunters don't camp in bands requiring three fires, Henrí," St. Paul pointed out in his usual pedantic manner.

Dumont bridled a bit at St. Paul's tone but kept his tongue.

Walking along the narrow path, St. Paul continued. "They hunt in the forest, but they don't risk burning them down in the summer." He checked his watch. "Nearly 0330 hours. Dawn will break in about two hours." He smelled rain on the wind from the east. "I want to get this done fast and get back on the road."

They walked through the woods. The nearest fire was behind the next thick stand of trees.

Dumont saw the glow growing brighter but still could not see who was around the fire. "What if there are many of them?"

The sergeant glanced back at his partner. "We'll be cautious, but I don't expect any problems." The closest fire was now clearly visible about fifty meters ahead. Several figures were gathered around it.

St. Paul motioned for his partner to move off to one side and cover him.

The veteran police officer wasn't expecting trouble. He followed a turn in the path past a thick bush. His night vision was degraded by looking toward the firelight. He missed a sudden movement close by when a man rose out of the brush immediately to his left. St. Paul automatically stepped back and reached for his pistol. He said, "Halt!" But his hand never reached the weapon. The point of a very sharp sword was under St. Paul's throat. It had happened in less than five seconds. Not daring to move, he turned his eyes to his right. To his dismay, he saw Dumont with another man holding a long spear pointed at his chest.

Sergeant Herbert St. Paul was no coward, but neither was he a fool. Shifting his gaze in both directions, he saw three more men holding swords or spears. And yet that wasn't the oddest thing about them. They were dressed like . . . Romans? Roman legionaries?

In moments more armed men appeared. The clearing was full of them.

The dark, beard-stubbled face of the man before him bore a look that was hostile and curious. His hair was long and unkempt, but he didn't look like a derelict drunk.

"Who the hell are you?" St. Paul asked carefully, trying to keep from touching the sword tip at his throat.

The man didn't reply but turned to his nearest companion with a questioning look. The other man shook his head and waved to someone else out of view. Then the man with the sword said something.

St. Paul felt a shiver run up his back. He had attended Catholic schools. He recognized the language. It was Latin.

They were herded at sword point toward the fire. The sergeant saw it had been used to roast several cuts from what appeared to be a large deer. It wasn't hunting season, but he decided to let that pass for the moment.

At least two hundred men gathered around the captives.

"What the hell is going on here, Sergeant?" Dumont whispered, not taking his eyes off the weapons pointed at him. "One of those dumb reenactments?" He tried to sound brave, but there was a note of hysteria in his voice.

St. Paul shook his head. "I don't know. Just remain calm and don't spook them."

Dumont leaned close. "What are we going to do?"

The older man didn't respond. He was looking at the Romans, noting their filthy tunics, rusty armor, long hair, and beards. Something very strange was going on here. He considered their options and chances of escape when Dumont interrupted him in a harsh whisper.

"Sergeant! Did you hear me?"

St. Paul shot him a look. "I heard you." He looked around them. At least ten men were close enough to be an immediate threat, and all were armed. "We will wait and see what happens. We are in no immediate danger."

"No immediate danger?" Dumont said with raised eyebrows. "Sergeant, there are hundreds of them. They have weapons and we're alone."

"I know. But other than bringing us here against our will, they have not threatened us." He saw the Romans around them part as three men approached. "It looks like we have company."

The three new arrivals wore elaborate armor. But their hair and beards were just as shaggy as the others. The one in the lead seemed to be in command. The second man was thin with a thoughtful expression on his narrow face. The third stood nearly a head taller than any other Roman with muscles that rippled under his red tunic. They stopped in front of St. Paul and Dumont. The first one, who was older than the others, faced St. Paul. "Who are you?"

Herbert St. Paul had a gift for languages, a useful skill in a country with many borders and cultures. In addition to his native Flemish, he spoke English, Dutch, French, and Italian. As a boy he had wanted to study for the priesthood. The Catholic school he'd attended in Antwerp still taught the old classical Latin, the language of scholars and clerics. Fortunately, it had been his best subject. "We are . . . law men," he replied cautiously. "And who are you?"

The older man's eyes widened. "You understand our language," he said. For some reason he showed relief at this.

St. Paul nodded.

"Excellent," the Roman officer said. "I am Legatus Lucius Cassius Aquilius, of Legio Fifty-four Vindicta. I need some questions answered."

St. Paul's own eyes grew wide at the officer's words. His memory of Latin was improving. Then he said in an authoritative voice, "You have committed a serious crime by bringing us here."

Lucius simply shrugged. "You came into our camp. My legionaries have orders to bring any intruders to me." Then his voice turned cold. "Consider yourselves fortunate. They also have orders to kill anyone they see as a threat."

The veteran Belgian police officer believed him. Having no choice, he decided to be diplomatic with these odd men. "Very well. I will answer what I can."

"First, we are in Belgicae. Who governs this region?"

Belgicae? "Well, the Belgian government, of course."

This caused the three men to exchange frowns. Lucius raised an eyebrow. "Is it not Rome who rules here?"

St. Paul almost laughed. "Of course not." Who are these people?

"I see," Lucius said, clearly disappointed.

"What is going on here?" St. Paul asked.

"You will address him as 'Sire!'" growled the tall one.

St. Paul's anger flared momentarily, but he quashed it. "Yes, Sire."

Lucius glanced at Marcus and back at St. Paul. "What year is this?"

St. Paul's mouth fell open. He had to have heard wrong. What year? "I do not think I heard you, Sire," he replied.

"I said, what year is this? What is the date?"

"2021."

This reply only caused perplexed looks among the three officers. "I do not understand that."

St. Paul realized he had answered in Flemish. He had to think for several seconds. He dimly recalled a bit of history from his classical education. Rome was founded in 753 BC, and all dates stemmed from that year. He did some quick mental calculations. 2774. He tried to recall how to say it in Latin. One hell of a time to forget that, he berated himself. But he had always been good with Roman numerals. "My apologies," he said. "Let me write it." He slowly pulled a notepad and pen from his jacket pocket and showed it to the officer.

"A stylus and slate is fine," said Lucius.

After clicking the pen, St. Paul wrote some figures, then showed the page to the other man.

Lucius, Marcus, and Septimus crowded closer to read the Roman numerals on the white paper. MMDCCLXXIV.

All three men gasped simultaneously, their eyes widening in horror.

"*De te perdent!*" Marcus said in disbelief. "Two thousand years?"

Lucius was staring at the numbers. How in the name of all the gods could it possibly be?

St. Paul had heard the exchange. It only deepened his confusion. The big one had cursed, then said, "two thousand years." Two thousand years what?

Lucius's dark eyes bored into St. Paul's. "Is this correct? This is the year? 2774?"

"Yes." Even if he'd been incorrect in his math, it didn't explain their reaction.

The officers began to talk rapidly among themselves, gesticulating with their hands. Most of the men nearby turned to watch the conversation.

Even with his rapidly improving Latin, St. Paul couldn't follow what they were saying. It was apparent the officers were upset at the information. He frowned, trying to figure out why they could be so agitated over the date. He wondered if they were a religious sect or some sort of Neo-Roman cult. Had they isolated themselves from society for many years? The Ardennes Forest was vast and dense, but it was inconceivable these men—and there appeared to be several hundred at least—could have hidden from the world for years.

Dumont leaned closer. "What are we going to do?"

The older officer looked at him, understanding his concern. "We're going to be patient, Henrí."

The patrolman wasn't to be put off. "They're distracted by whatever you told them. We can draw our guns and make them back off. We have to call for backup."

St. Paul had to admit the time for escape was ripe, but he was not sure they'd get away. "Henrí, we wouldn't get ten meters."

"But we still have our pistols."

St. Paul looked at the three officers, still in agitated conversation. In his years as a policeman, he had become adept at sensing when someone was telling the truth or a lie. He could tell when someone was putting on an act.

They were not acting. He turned to Dumont. "Let me ask you something. Who do you think they are?" He gestured to the Romans around him.

"I don't know, a group of renegade reenactors or some cult that worships Caesar? Who cares?"

"I do. I want to know who they are. And I think they'll tell me."

Dumont reached for his holstered pistol. "We can make them tell us—"

"Don't touch your weapon!" St. Paul hissed. "If they see you . . ." He stopped. Several Romans had seen Dumont's movement, but not one reacted. In fact, they didn't seem to care that their captives carried loaded firearms. He frowned. "Remain still. I want to try something." He slowly lifted the flap on his holster, slid the pistol out, and held it at his front in plain sight. The movement should have warranted a protest or question.

But the Romans simply did not seem to care or even notice a loaded weapon held by a man being held against his will. "Damn," he said in a low voice. "I don't believe it."

"Don't they see it?" Dumont was equally surprised.

"Yes. They simply don't seem to care. I've never seen anything like it."

"So let's get out of here." Dumont reached for his sidearm.

"Dumont!" St. Paul snapped. "I told you not to touch your weapon. I will not repeat myself. There is something very odd going on here." He looked at a Roman standing close by, listening to the discussion between the commanders. He appeared to be in his late twenties, and his helmet bore a bedraggled white crest. "That one is a centurion," he said. "I'm going to ask him."

"What makes you think he'll tell you?" said Dumont.

"He is younger than the others." He smiled at the officer. "Centurio, may I speak with you?"

The officer turned to see the man with the strange clothing addressing him. He moved closer. "Yes?"

"What is your name?"

"Pompaius Sestus, Cohort Apollo." Sestus was unsure he should be talking to the intruders, but perhaps he might learn something useful to the legatus. "What do you want?"

St. Paul tried to look as guileless as possible, even though he was holding a loaded firearm. "Your leader seems upset at what I told him. Can you tell me why?"

Sestus regarded the man for a long moment. "We have just learned it has been two thousand years since we last saw the sun. We were only to be in the cellar for a decade, perhaps a few more years." Sestus was clearly upset. "But something went wrong with the alchemist's plan."

St. Paul tried to grasp what the younger man was saying but decided the details could wait. "Centurio, we mean you no harm. Perhaps we can help you to return to Rome."

Sestus shook his head. "We are not going to Rome. We have another duty, one that we have long waited to fulfill."

"What duty is that?"

Sestus looked as if he were about to answer but caught himself. His voice became hard. "I may not tell you this. You are intruders into our camp. You may be scouts of our enemies."

The veteran police officer backed off. "I understand. I apologize." Then he saw Lucius coming over with the other two officers. Sestus turned to the older man. "Sire, this one has been asking questions of me. I have not given him any information."

Lucius gave the younger officer a supportive smile. "Well done, Sestus." Then he looked at St. Paul. "Are there any armies or forts near here or to the east? Before the Rhenus River, that is?"

St. Paul frowned. He knew the information wasn't classified, but he hedged his words. "Why do you want to know?"

The tall man next to Lucius stepped forward, but Lucius held up his hand. "He is doing his duty, Marcus." After a moment he said, "We must be sure we will not run across any forts or camps that may impede us in our march."

"Can you tell me where you are going?" The Rhenus, or Rhine River, was the border with Germany. But why were these men going there?

Then Lucius answered. "We are the remains of a legion who have recently arisen from deathly slumber in a cellar in Gallicae to seek vengeance on our Germanic enemies."

For several seconds St. Paul said nothing. Then he found his voice. "I, ah . . . did I hear you correctly, Sire?"

Lucius nodded. "I believe you did. And we are only now beginning to see how long it has been for us." Lucius looked at the men around them.

The police sergeant struggled to clear his head. "What year did you uh . . . begin your campaign?"

"We, that is, the entire legion, put ourselves in the Somnum in the year 767 in the reign of Emperor Gaius Augustus."

St. Paul went silent as Lucius went back to talk to the other officers. Dumont nudged his superior. "What did he say?"

After a moment St. Paul told him.

"That's totally impossible. They are crazy or delusional. Maybe on drugs."

That had occurred to St. Paul. But no, somehow, and he could not imagine how, this was real.

"We have to get out of here," Dumont pressed.

The older officer cocked his head. "I'm open to a logical suggestion." Logic would be a nice change, he mused silently.

"We could point our weapons at them."

Sergeant St. Paul turned on his partner. "You do not seem to get it. These people don't know what a gun is."

Dumont looked puzzled. "How is that possible? They have to be reenactors or something."

"I don't agree. I've seen some of those reenactor groups. They're very fastidious about their equipment and armor. It's extremely expensive. Look at them. Their armor is tarnished, even rusty. No historical group would take such poor care of their equipment." He paused, gathering his thoughts. "And the way they hardly even notice I'm openly holding a firearm. It doesn't make sense."

A slight narrowing of the eyes was Dumont's reaction. "So what are you saying? That these are real Romans, come back from the grave?" He was almost sneering, clearly on the edge of doing something rash.

"Well, they obviously think so," St. Paul said, glancing at the Romans. "There is something strange about them, and we need to find out before we go shooting our way out. I don't believe they know what a firearm is."

"If we fired at them, they would."

This was exactly what St. Paul did not want to hear from his partner. "We're not in immediate danger. Shooting one is not justified."

"We could fire in the air," Dumont said.

"No," the sergeant said. "If I'm right, they would hear a loud bang and see a flash. But what will it mean to them?"

"That we have weapons."

St. Paul sighed. "You're not thinking. Just say for the sake of argument that these people have never in their lives ever even heard of firearms."

Dumont shrugged reluctantly. "Okay."

"So you fire in the air. They might shout or jump, but when it's over, they don't see anything except you holding a strange tool that makes noise and fire."

"But . . ." the patrolman said dubiously.

"Firearms weren't developed until several hundred years after the fall of Rome. They have absolutely no concept of what a gun is. You can't explain bullets to them any more than I could explain television to a caveman."

"You think they're real Romans," Dumont said, looking at his sergeant with unconcealed scorn.

St. Paul glared at him. "I order you to remain as you are, Patrolman Dumont. Do you hear me?" A curt nod was his answer. "I'm going to call for backup."

He reached for his radio, then stopped himself. What in the world was he going to say? "Dispatch, we're in the woods with several hundred Romans from the first century AD. Can you send some Visigoths and barbarians for backup?" He almost chuckled at the idea. His thoughts were interrupted by Dumont.

"What are you going to say?"

"I was thinking the same thing," he replied. "I can't very well tell the truth, can I?"

"So don't give specifics. Just say there's a large number of armed men in the forest, and we need strong, armed backup."

That was a logical answer, and it raised his recently dropped opinion of Dumont. Just a notch. "Good thinking. We can sort out the details later." Again he reached for the small radio on his belt. Sestus looked at him curiously but did not react. Using Dumont to shield his movements, St. Paul turned the volume down to nearly the bottom of the scale and put his mouth close to the pickup. He keyed the "Transmit" button. "Dispatch, this is Patrol 37. Do you read? Over."

"Patrol 37, dispatch. What is your status? Over." The woman's voice sounded alarmingly loud to him, but he had it almost to his ear. It could not have carried more than a few meters. Sestus glanced at him but did nothing.

"Dispatch, Patrol 37. We are in sector 11-92, about three klicks west of Boullion Road, in the woods. We have encountered a large group of armed men. We are heavily outnumbered and need immediate and strong backup. Do you copy? Over." He waited, envisioning the reaction his words must be generating at headquarters in Bastogne. He winced as a man's voice cut in. "Patrol 37, amplify. A large group of armed men? How many and how armed, over?" It was the loud voice of Kurt Hoster, the pugnacious senior watch officer for the night shift. At least Marina, the dispatcher, knew enough to keep her voice down.

"Repeat, we are being held by a large number of armed men in uniform. Cannot ascertain weapon types but consider this force to be hostile, over."

"I need more to go on than that before I call out the troops, 37," Hoster said acidly. "They're probably our army on night maneuvers."

Idiot! St. Paul fumed. "I would know the uniform, Dispatch. I wore it for six years. They are not our troops, nor French. Over."

"That leaves American or German. And they are members of NATO, 37. I'd look like a fool if I called in a response on our own troops."

"They are not NATO troops," St. Paul said flatly. "Over."

"Then what uniform are they wearing? Over."

St. Paul almost groaned in frustration. "I don't recognize the uniform. This is a serious armed intrusion across our border." Then he had a thought and leaned over to Dumont. "Get your phone and shoot some pictures."

"Got it." Dumont yanked a mobile phone from his pocket and held it up. None of the Romans did more than look at him. "Okay," he said. "I'll send them to Headquarters."

"Good man," St. Paul said. "Dispatch, Patrol 37. We're sending some photos of the intruders. But you must move fast, over."

"Very well, 37. Stand by for—" The radio was suddenly snatched from his hand by Sestus, who'd silently come up behind him. The young officer was holding the radio with an expression of wonder on his face. They heard Hoster's voice again. "Patrol 37! Do you copy? Respond immediately! Over."

Sestus almost dropped the talking thing in surprise but ran toward Lucius and Marcus, who were in a heated debate with Septimus.

"Sires," Sestus said loudly. "You must see this!"

"What is it?" Marcus said.

"One of the strangers was talking at this thing." Sestus held the object out. "Sire, it talked back at him!"

Lucius frowned. "What do you mean, 'it talked?'" He took the small thing from Sestus.

Hoster answered for him. "Patrol 37! This is dispatch! Reply immediately and report your status!" He was so loud that St. Paul and Dumont heard him clearly from ten meters away.

"Patrol 37, you must—" Hoster's voice was cut off as Lucius ran his fingers over the strange object, pushing the plastic buttons.

"What is it?" Lucius said with wide eyes. "Is there a spirit inside this thing? Is it haunted?"

"I do not know, Sire," Septimus replied, clearly fascinated.

"Patrol 37. Repeat that. I did not copy. Over!" Hoster was shouting as if that would work when mere radio waves failed.

"Idiot!" St. Paul growled to himself. *What do we do now?* He didn't notice when Dumont slid his pistol out of the holster and flicked off the safety. A thin smile crept across the patrolman's lips. Then he raised the pistol and pointed it at Lucius.

"You're all under arrest by the authority of the State Police. Drop your weapons and lie face down on the ground!"

St. Paul was stunned. It had happened so fast he hadn't been able to react. The fact that Dumont had deliberately disobeyed him was moot. He had his weapon out and was brandishing it in a manner that no one, not even a first-century Roman could fail to recognize as threatening. "Dumont!" he snapped, watching the Romans, who were all staring at Dumont. "Don't move!"

"I'm not listening to you, Sergeant. You're not rational. I'm taking charge of this situation."

St. Paul saw several legionaries holding swords and spears coming at Dumont. Instinctively he brought his own pistol up and stepped back.

Dumont saw they were heavily outnumbered and pointed the Walther pistol at first one Roman, then another. "Halt. I warn you. Halt!"

He's losing it, St. Paul thought, desperate to stop the accelerating danger.

Dumont's hands were shaking. "I said halt! Stand back and put down your weapons or I will fire." St. Paul heard the quaver in Dumont's voice.

The nearest Roman reached out and grabbed Dumont's pistol and pulled. With his fingers wrapped tightly around the grip and trigger, Dumont tried to pull back.

An ear-shattering blast and yellow flash made all the Romans jump in shock. A gout of reddish-pink vapor erupted from the Roman's back, glittering in the firelight. He was instantly knocked back as if by an immense fist and fell in a twitching heap at Dumont's feet.

Dumont stared at the dead man in horror.

Then another Roman threw his spear. The barbed shaft stabbed into Dumont's chest and emerged from his back. The young patrolman staggered and fired wildly in reflex. He looked down and saw the shaft projecting from his body, a dark stain spreading across his jacket. Another Roman shoved his sword into Henrí Dumont's stomach, slicing him open before withdrawing the bloody weapon. Dumont dropped to his knees and fell backward. He was dying even as his body hit the ground.

St. Paul knew he was doomed as the crowd of angry Romans closed in about him. In Latin he told them to halt. He aimed and fired at the nearest man, who fell screaming in pain. Then he fired again and again, the muzzle blasts strobing like yellow lightning on the Roman armor. Three more went down. Sergeant Herbert St. Paul felt the searing, burning pressure as a spear entered his body. Then another came at him, and he felt only a blinding shock. He fell onto his back. The world spun around him. There was no pain. His last sight was of Lucius standing over him with a look of sadness on his face.

Sergeant Herbert St. Paul's last thought was that the Roman was crying, but it was only rain falling from the dark skies.

CHAPTER VIII

ENIGMAS

At eight o'clock Monday morning, the NATO Legal Services Department met for their weekly conference.

Braden entered the long windowless conference room ten minutes early and saw Joan Bannister, Barney Rabble, Stuart Wainwright, and Brent Matthews already sitting at the long table. Jonathan Howard's executive assistant Charlene Myers came in, smiling at Braden. "Good morning, Alex. Did you and Ann have a nice weekend?"

"We sure did," he replied as she flipped open her notebook computer. "I'm sure Ann can give you a better description than I can."

Charlene's blue eyes twinkled. "She did. She called me last night and told me about the maze. You're so sneaky."

Braden grinned. "Did she mention anything else?"

She gave him a look that clearly said, "You'll never know."

He sighed and went over to a counter by the door. On it was a large Keurig coffee maker and a plate of fresh pastries. He selected a French Roast and waited for the machine to finish brewing, then added cream and a packet of sugar. Say what you like about duty in Belgium, he thought, but we get the best coffee and pastries in the world. As he put two cheese Danish rolls on a plate, he heard the rumble of distant thunder beyond the walls. The storm had started the night before and was still coming down in buckets when he'd pulled into his numbered parking space. The European Weather Network had been predicting a series of summer rainstorms to pass over the Rhine River Valley, Belgium, and eastern France in the next week.

He sat down next to Joan, a stout New Englander with copper-colored hair in a tight bun that accented her businesslike manner. Joan took her job seriously, which made her one of the best legal advisors in NATO.

"Good morning, Joan," Braden said, smiling and sipping the rich coffee.

"Good morning to you, Alex," she said with a quick look up from her reading.

He would have asked about her weekend, but Joan wasn't one for small talk. She ran the German office, and it was clear she had a lot on her mind.

His closest friend Barney Rabble was sitting across from him, fiddling with his gold Cross pen. "Hey, Al," the short blond man said, glancing at the clock. It was three minutes to eight.

Howard's going to be late, Braden thought. *For once I win the bet.*

"Nice weekend?" the legal advisor to the French office asked him.

"Great, Barn," Braden said. "You?"

"Worked most of it." Barney Rabble actually bore a slight resemblance to the *Flintstones* cartoon character, being short and stout with a wedge of blonde hair jutting over his forehead. Despite the ribbing he'd endured all his life, Rabble had a superb legal mind and analytical skill that would have made Sherlock Holmes feel insecure. He was an authority on early television animation and owned one of the most extensive collections of rare Hanna-Barbera animation cels in private hands. He was still gazing at the wall clock. "Hmm. Twenty seconds to go."

Braden shot him a wicked smile. "Get your wallet out."

Rabble merely cocked his head. "There's still time." Just as the second hand touched the eleven on the clock, Jonathan Howard swept into the conference room like a gray-haired Texas tornado. He sat in his chair at the head of the table. Charlene had his coffee ready.

Braden rolled his eyes, pulled a five-euro bill from his pocket, and flipped it across the table to Rabble who took it with a grin. "Won't you ever learn? He never misses."

Braden sighed. "I'll win someday." Then he regarded their boss. Howard seemed overly tense. I wonder what happened over the weekend? A momentary image of a nude Ann relaxing in a black marble bathtub intruded on his mind, and he forced it away.

"Let's get started," Howard said curtly in his deep voice. "We have a lot to cover. This German crisis is getting worse, and we need to be on top of it. You're on, Ms. Bannister."

"Thank you, John," Joan said. "As I'm sure you're all aware, the current mood of the German people, in particular those under fifty, are pushing for Chancellor Hoffman to support a German withdrawal from NATO by the first of the year. This is serious. The largest and most powerful continental member is considering leaving the alliance."

Braden spoke up. "Chancellor Hoffman is very pro-NATO. How is he holding up?"

Joan turned to him. "Not bad, considering. So far, the majority opinion is on our side. The over-fifty age group makes up ninety percent of the voters." She leafed through some papers.

"But things are heating up. There have been a lot of protests by anti-NATO groups and isolated political extremists, particularly in Central Germany and Bavaria. Some have become violent, resulting in arrests, injuries, and three deaths."

Those in the room absorbed this. Joan went on. "The most serious incidents involved isolated attacks on NATO personnel, particularly Americans. So far, they appear to be impulsive acts rather than organized. But all regimental commanders have issued orders that soldiers are not to travel in groups of less than five. We're watching for any sign of violence on military personnel in other member nations."

Howard cut in. "That's why we all need to be in on this matter. If the violence spreads to other NATO nations, it may indicate a larger anti-NATO movement in Europe." He looked at Stuart Wainwright, the newest member of the department. "Spain has a history of fascism, and it may crop up there next."

Wainwright's pale face seemed to turn even whiter at the sudden attention he received from around the table. "Yes, sir," he managed to say. "I'll check with my Spanish counterparts."

"Good. I'll talk to Leslie Crouch when she returns from Rome. She needs to keep her Italian correspondents up to date for the same reason."

Joan resumed. "In any case, the big news is the anti-NATO protests in Germany." She handed out printouts of Internet news stories.

Braden scanned the pages. The first large protest lasted three days and involved over five hundred people. It had been in Munich, a breeding ground for extreme political movements, including National Socialism. Over twenty people had been arrested but later released by court order. Protests in Frankfurt am Main and Stuttgart had again led to police involvement. No one had been prosecuted. All had been released within twenty-four hours of their arrest.

Frowning, Braden turned his attention to Joan, who had waited for everyone to finish reading.

"Hoffman is taking a stand based on the good relationship with NATO," she said. "He is planning a series of rallies and media events intended to show the advantages of the long alliance with NATO."

Rabble leaned forward. "That's a start. But can Poland or the Czech Republic influence the decision in our favor? Or any of the Balkan states?"

"Yes and no," Joan answered. "The former Warsaw Pact nations bordering Germany are leery of a resurgence of any overt German nationalism, as you can imagine. Greece, Turkey, and Albania don't want to get involved. They have their own issues with the Middle East."

"Anyone else?" asked Wainwright.

"France, Italy, the United States, and Britain are putting some pressure on the Hoffman Cabinet to shelve the resolution for another four-year session. Hoffman is popular and holding the line. For now, at least."

Howard sipped his coffee. "The secretary-general is meeting with him tomorrow."

Joan continued. "The real core of the problem are the Germans born after 1955, who make up roughly sixty-four percent of the population. They do not see the need to stay in an organization founded by invaders and run by conquerors. They say the Cold War is over, that Russia is no longer a threat."

The men and women around the table said nothing for a long moment. Then Howard leaned forward. "The younger ones strongly object to NATO basing foreign troops in Germany." He paused. "And a small faction resents the influx of non-German races into the country, investing foreign money and building foreign-owned businesses."

"Aw, crap," Rabble said, shaking his head. "Won't they ever learn? That should have died out after the Holocaust."

No one disagreed. Aryan purity was always a deep-rooted matter to many Germans, if not publicly so. The fall of Nazism had smothered that particular fire, but it had not been put out entirely. Racism was still present but expressed more discreetly.

Howard leaned back in his chair and rubbed his chin. "Since the breakup of the Soviet Union and the reunification of Germany, they have decided that Germany no longer needs the protection of NATO." He snorted. "They've forgotten there are still dragons in the world, and those dragons aren't always big and noisy like the Russians." Howard, a former Austin prosecutor, often betrayed his Texas conservatism in his speech. "Idiots," he muttered. "If we lose Germany, we all lose."

There were many active terrorist groups in the world, and a goodly percentage of them were based in Europe. So far, no attacks as bad as 9/11 had happened, but there had been bombings in Bonn, Berlin, Brussels, London, Leipzig, Paris, Athens, Prague, and Rome, with hundreds killed and wounded. NATO's job of keeping the peace had become much more complicated.

"Bottom line," Howard said with barely concealed disdain, "they want a withdrawal of all American Army and Air Force personnel, all logistical and technical support units, and equipment. If that happens, then we'll lose most of the bases, roads, rail transport, and logistics for military operations in Europe. NATO will be strong, but it will have one hell of a huge hole in the middle."

Heads nodded at this.

"But don't they realize," Braden said, "they would be limiting our ability to assist them in case of a terrorist attack? The latest threat is from radical Islamic fundamentalists. Some of them want Europe back as it had been before the Crusades. And they've proven they don't mind killing hundreds of innocent people to do it. Germany is one of their prime targets."

Howard rubbed his eyes. "They'll still have our support. Having their cake and eating it too, so to speak." He looked at Joan. Anything else on this?"

She shook her head.

"Okay, I'll keep you all informed. But if there are any matters pertaining to the German situation that crop up in your own cases, I would like to be told immediately." Everyone showed their assent. Then Howard picked up a folder and opened it. "This morning a strange report came in concerning the Belgian State Police. Apparently, it has a military aspect to it that could involve NATO." He looked down the table to a handsome black man seated past Joan. "Brent, can you fill us in on the details?"

"Certainly," said Brent Matthews in a deep, resonant voice. An investigator like Braden, he worked the Belgian desk. Putting on a pair of gold-rimmed glasses, he tapped on his iPad. "At 0312 hours this morning, the State Police headquarters in Bastogne received a transmission from two officers, Sergeant Herbert St. Paul and Patrolman Henrí Dumont, on night patrol north of Boullion. They radioed they had discovered some campfires in the woods near the French border." He looked down the table. "Open fires are illegal in the summer."

Rabble frowned. "Fires? In the rain?"

"It was before the rain hit that area," Matthews explained. "At 0335, they called in, saying that they had encountered a 'large group of armed men' in the forest at coordinates 11-92 and needed 'immediate and strong backup.'"

Braden cut in. "Did they say what weapons they carried?"

Matthews shook his head. "No, there were no details."

Braden watched Rabble folding the euro into complex shapes. He often played with origami when deep in thought. But Braden knew he was absorbing every word.

"Sorry to interrupt," Braden said. "Go on."

"This is where it gets weird," Matthews said. "The night watch commander, Captain Hoster, asked for details. A moment later, they heard some strange words in a different voice than St. Paul's. No one could understand what was said." There were a few raised eyebrows around the table. Matthews continued. "Hoster tried to reestablish contact, but there was no response. He finally ordered a squad of twenty officers with automatic weapons and riot gear to head for the coordinates."

Only the tapping of Charlene's fingers on her laptop keyboard broke the silence.

"At 0453 hours, they found the patrol car on the Boullion Road. It was raining hard by then. They headed for Sector 11-92 and reached it at approximately 0513 hours. But there was no sign of St. Paul or Dumont. All they found were the remains of three campfires and the butchered carcass of a deer. But it was obvious a large group had been in the area."

Rabble appeared to be fully absorbed in his origami. He spoke up. "Okay. Let me see if I got this. The second call came in at 0335, but the backup units didn't get there until 0513?"

"Right," Matthews said.

"That's ninety-eight minutes. What took them so long?"

"Bastogne is about seventy klicks from 11-92. The storm grounded their response helicopters. They went in three vans."

"Okay," Rabble said, still folding the bill. "But an hour and a half isn't much time for a large group of men to disappear. Were they able to determine which way they went?"

"It had been raining hard before the searchers found the car. The rain erased most of the footprints. They estimated that at least three hundred men, probably more, had been there and cooked some game. Their route in was difficult to determine, as was egress from the site. Just after dawn, another team of investigators arrived and took over. They're still at the site. The latest report, which I read just as I came in this morning, is that they found several bloodstains in the mud near one of the fires."

Howard grimaced. "Hell. Any sign of St. Paul or Dumont?"

"Not so far," Matthews replied. "The response team began a search of the general vicinity. They're on foot. All helicopters are grounded until the storm lifts."

Howard shook his head. "That won't be easy. The Ardennes Forest around there is as thick as quills on a porcupine's ass."

There were a few smiles at Howard's words, but no one disagreed.

"Does Bastogne have any idea who the men were?" Braden asked.

Matthews again accessed his iPad. "I'll read you the transcript. We have a recording, but it's in Flemish, of course. I know some of us aren't fluent in it." Wainwright and two others shook their heads.

"Okay." He cleared his throat. "I'll leave out all the 'overs' and stuff. St. Paul first calls in. 'Dispatch, this is Patrol 37.' Then the Bastogne dispatcher answered, 'Patrol 37, what is your status?' St. Paul replied, 'We are in sector 11-92, about three klicks west of Boullion Road, in the woods. We have encountered a large group of armed men. We are heavily outnumbered and need immediate and strong backup.'"

Braden saw intense interest on everyone's face. Only Rabble seemed disinterested. That meant he wasn't missing a single word.

Matthews continued. "Hoster took the microphone at this point. 'Patrol 37, amplify. A large group of armed men? How many and how armed?' St. Paul responded with, 'Repeat, we are being held by a large number of armed men in uniform. Cannot ascertain weapon types, but consider this force to be hostile.'"

Matthews tapped the iPad screen and resumed. "Hoster then said, 'I need more to go on than that before I call out the troops, 37. They're probably our army on night maneuvers.' St. Paul said, 'I would know the uniform, Dispatch. I wore it for six years. They are not our troops, nor French.'"

"He was a former soldier?" Joan asked.

"Yeah. Six years with the army. Made corporal. Good record." He returned his attention to the iPad. "Hoster replied, 'That leaves American or German. And they are members of NATO, 37. I'd look like a fool if I called in a response on our own troops.'"

Rabble shook his head at the obtuse response. Braden saw his friend's lips formed the word "asshole."

"St. Paul said, 'They are not NATO troops.' Hoster: 'Then what uniform are they wearing?'"

Everyone leaned closer to hear what St. Paul had said next. "'I don't recognize the uniform. This is a serious armed intrusion across our border.' Then St. Paul told them, 'Dispatch, we are sending some photos of the intruders. But you must move fast.' Then Hoster said, 'Very well, 37. Stand by for orders. We will be back to you as soon as we see the pictures.'" Matthews looked up from the iPad to see the others watching him intently. "At that point, something must have happened. In Bastogne, they heard at least three squelch breaks. What Hoster said was cut off. Then Hoster became agitated and demanded St. Paul respond." He paused. "But the next voice wasn't St. Paul's. It was at least two other men speaking a strange language."

"And then what?" Howard asked.

Matthews consulted the iPad. "Then they heard Dumont speaking, 'You're all under arrest by the authority of the State Police. Drop your weapons and lie face down on the ground! Do as I say, now!' He sounded like he was about to panic."

Matthews clicked a page forward. "Then St. Paul said 'Dumont! Don't move!' Dumont replied, 'I'm not listening to you, Sergeant. You are not rational. I'm taking charge of this situation. I order you to stand back and put down your weapons, or I will be forced to fire.'" Matthews put down the iPad. "The next thing they heard was a gunshot. A few minutes later was a brief conversation in that same unknown language. That was it."

For several seconds no one spoke. Then Howard looked around the table. "Any comments?"

"It's odd," said Rabble in a clinical voice. "Dumont challenged his superior officer and took matters into his own hands."

"Yeah," Braden said. "That must be when things got out of control."

Rabble said, "Dumont said, 'You are not rational.' That indicates St. Paul was doing something unusual."

"What kind of officer was St. Paul?" asked Joan.

Matthews checked his iPad. "Sergeant St. Paul was a veteran of the army and fifteen years with the State Police. Excellent record, very well regarded. Three citations for excellent performance from the state. Dumont was a rookie. Three months' duty."

"St. Paul doesn't seem to be the type to make mistakes," Howard pointed out.

Rabble nodded. "Whatever was going on, Dumont felt he had to take control of the situation. At least one shot was fired. Contact was lost. We can assume both officers are dead or incapacitated."

No one disagreed with this.

"But who did it?" Joan Bannister asked.

Rabble didn't look at her but continued folding the euro. "It's curious that Bastogne didn't recognize the language. Belgian State Police officers are usually fluent in French, English, Dutch, and German. It stands to reason someone there would know it."

"Right," agreed Matthews. "But this wasn't any of those."

"That *is* weird," Braden agreed. "Are they looking into any of the Arabic or Slavic languages?"

Matthews nodded. "Of course. Nothing so far."

"Arabic?" Rabble looked at Braden pointedly. "Are you thinking Islamic terrorists?" He put the folded euro on the table.

"Aren't we all?" Braden saw it had been folded into a unicorn, complete with horn. He smiled inwardly. Rabble had a sense of symbolism.

Wainwright spoke up. "What about the pictures?"

"Oh yeah," said Matthews. He slid two printed images from a folder. "Here. See what you make of them."

Braden reached for one. It was clearly taken using a mobile phone. All he could see were about ten figures silhouetted in front of the glow of a campfire. They appeared to be barelegged and wore something bulky on their upper torsos, but no other details were visible. "Shit," he said, exchanging the picture with the one Rabble held. This one was no better and showed three men, apparently talking. One of the figures was taller than the other two. "They appear to be wearing something bulky on their torsos," he said.

"Body armor," Rabble said absently. "Possibly military or police."

"What about using Photoshop to bring out the images?" Braden asked.

"I'll send them to Charlie in the graphics lab," Matthews replied. "Anyway, there was no further contact. The recording is being analyzed. We should know more later today."

Howard looked at the photos. "Are there any indications this is an unannounced military exercise by the Belgians or the French?"

"None," Matthews said. "I checked. No army or special operations unit is scheduled for maneuvers at this time. I'm betting it's not the Germans or Dutch, either. This is not a military event. Not a friendly one, that is."

No one had anything to say, even Rabble.

Howard slid the photos back to Matthews. "Okay. Now on to regular business. Let's start with you, Alex. Can you fill us in on your cases?"

"Sure, John," Braden said and turned on his own iPad. Back to normality.

André Robert glared at what he saw around him. For fifty meters in every direction were empty chardonnay vines, stripped of their valuable fruit. "Who the hell did this? They're not ready!" Finding one plant that still had some remaining grapes, he plucked one and squeezed the sweet pulp onto his tongue. "Damn!" The chardonnay was still at least a month away from being ready for picking. But someone had stripped at least ten percent of the prizewinning vintage. His workers were tending the Beaujolais and Bordeaux vines two kilometers to the east. But he knew who was responsible. "That useless Antonio," he hissed. "I told him no picking was to be done until I approved it."

Antonio Cavarelli was married to Robert's only daughter, Fiona. He had been supervising the winery while Robert recovered from his persistent summer cold. Fiona had insisted her father remain in bed. It had been nearly ten days since he had been able to walk his vineyards. The well-meaning but ineffectual Italian had given his father-in-law daily reports on the status of his vineyards and workers. "I should have known better than to trust a stockbroker," he said sourly. "And here is the proof. At least a hundred cases gone. Those grapes won't even be good enough for a California wine."

After pulling out a handkerchief and blowing his nose, he resumed walking between the tall wooden racks supporting the denuded chardonnay vines. He scuffed the dry soil with his boot. Fortunately, the storm that had been hammering Belgium wasn't forecast to come this far west. A heavy rain this late in the season could damage the grapes.

He was not far from where he had been clearing more acreage. The same day the sinkhole had opened and almost swallowed him, he recalled.

Then he stopped at the last row of empty vines. In the fine soil, he saw dozens, no, hundreds of footprints. Leaning over, he peered at the marks. They weren't the prints of work shoes or boots. They looked more like some kind of soft sandal print. Some had hobnail patterns in them. So it hadn't been his workers. He felt only a little better. Someone else had managed to steal over three hundred square meters of his best grape harvest. It enraged Robert, and he paused to calm himself as he looked past the vines on the western edge of his vineyard. Past the denuded area was the shallow pit of the sinkhole he'd broken open. The wide depression was surrounded by stakes and rope. To his right, the land sloped down into a grassy hollow to a small stream.

Robert decided to go down to the stream and take a few moments to think about his late wife, Marie, who he missed greatly since her death from cancer the previous year. A wooden bench set close to the water was her favorite place to read and relax.

The thick trees cast deep purple shade along the stream. He placed a hand on the wooden backrest, feeling the cold wood slats under his fingers. Visions of Marie flooded his mind's eye; her love of quiet reflection and classic literature. It was cool in the glade, and the dirt along the small stream was moist under his boots.

Then he saw more footprints. He knew hikers sometimes rested by the stream. Marie hadn't minded unless she wanted to be alone. But this was different. A large area had been trodden by several dozen feet. Robert bent down and saw two clear prints on the muddy bank. They faced the water. Apparently, someone had knelt to scoop up water or wash their hands. But the great number of prints puzzled him. Robert followed the trail up the side of the deep vale. As he emerged into the sunlight, he stopped. His pale blue eyes widened in surprise.

An area nearly twenty meters in width was trampled by what had to have been hundreds of feet. "*Merde*," Robert exclaimed, seeing the remains of what had once been a pristine hillside of high grass. It was now a trodden scar on his land. It wasn't that it had been destroyed; it would grow back. But the fact that so many people had invaded his land and stolen from him disturbed André Robert.

"Antonio wouldn't recognize an invasion unless he heard about it on the Internet," he growled, knowing he was being unfair. Antonio tried hard, but he didn't have much common sense and no understanding of the ways of people and the real world. He was more concerned with computers and making money. Well, there wasn't anything wrong with making money, was there? But there was something wrong with the idea of making it over wires and through monitor screens instead of harvesting grapes to make God's nectar.

He could not do anything about the lost grapes, but he didn't dare leave his precious vineyard in the care of his inept son-in-law. Then he trudged back up the trail, which wound past a short, steep hillside. He stopped in wonderment and increasing anger. Normally covered in low brush and thick grass, the base of the hill had a huge pile of dead yellow grass piled against it. The trail of footprints ended at its base. He grasped a handful of the dry grass and tossed it aside. He saw not soil but . . . wood. Exposed in the sunlight was a thick dark plank of old wood.

"What in Heaven's name is that doing there?" Robert said aloud. He shoved more dead grass aside and saw more planks of the same dark wood, set edge to edge. It looked like a big trapdoor set into the hillside. He tugged the edge of the nearest board. It was heavy and resisted his efforts to get a grip on it. He pulled out his vintner's knife and jammed the thick blade under the edge of one board. Then he levered it up, finally securing a grip on one side. It was over six centimeters thick and heavy as hell. He wheezed at the effort. He hadn't fully recovered from his cold.

After shoving the thick plank to one side, he wiped the sweat from his forehead.

Before him was a black, bottomless tunnel into the hillside.

"*Incroyable.*"

CHAPTER IX

BLOODLINES

"You found a what?" Fiona Cavarelli looked at her father with a puzzled expression on her face.

"I told you," Robert said to her in exasperation. "It was a hole, a large hole in the hillside. I pulled the boards away and found a tunnel leading down into the earth. I couldn't see the bottom, but it was lined with dressed stone and had steps." He shook his head. "It was under the chardonnay vines. Over three hundred square meters of the vines had been picked. Stripped of what would have been my best vintage of the year."

"Who picked them, Papa?"

Robert shook his head. "How the hell should I know? Not a good vintner, that's for sure. Those grapes are not ready. But I think whoever put that pit on my land did it." He was annoyed that Fiona was having so much difficulty grasping the importance of what he'd found. He was standing in the living room of his home where he and Marie had lived for thirty years. Fiona and Antonio had been staying there while he was sick. Antonio, a swarthy Neapolitan with short black hair and soft skin, glanced at his wife with a worried expression. Apparently, he'd failed to notice this glaring intrusion on the land or the stripping of a large portion of the chardonnay vines.

"But how did it get there, Papa?" Fiona asked in a calming voice.

"I don't know," Robert sighed. "I've never seen it before, and neither had my father or grandfather." He sat down in his favorite chair next to the one Marie had used. Robert rubbed his chin, ignoring the dirt smudge on his stubbled jaw. "I think it's a Roman cellar," finally voicing his inner thoughts.

"A what?" Antonio asked, speaking for the first time. He was a bit afraid of his redoubtable father-in-law.

Robert stared at him with a frown. "What kind of an Italian are you? A Roman cellar, for God's sake! The Romans." He raised an eyebrow. "Surely you've heard of them."

The younger man's dark eyes flashed at that, but his wife patted his arm. "Of course I have, Papa," he said. "But what exactly is a Roman cellar?"

Robert took a pad of paper from a small table at his side and slid a pencil from a pocket. "It's a large underground cellar with storerooms," he explained, sketching out a rough diagram on the pad. He drew a hallway intersected at intervals with rooms. "A few have been found in the region. The Romans built them to store supplies and equipment. Some vintners use them to store and age the best champagne and wines for years. They're old as hell, more than a thousand years, and still in perfect shape. Most of them held up even under two world wars. Some are tourist attractions." He remembered his increasing glee at the discovery, knowing what he had to have found and what it meant. Riches and prosperity for his winery and his family. Even Antonio. Oh, well . . .

The public would be drawn by the discovery of a Roman cellar possibly containing artifacts and even wealth. The archaeologists and historians would be the first. Once they'd explored the site and learned all there was to learn, then would come the tourists with money and a zest for the fine wines and champagnes aged to perfection in a real Roman ruin.

And it was all on his land. His. He might even open up a small museum, depending on what was found inside. Marie would be so proud of him. He might even name it after her.

"So what will you do about it, Papa?" Fiona's voice cut into his empire-building.

He looked at her for a long moment. There was one problem. Someone knew about the cellar. It had been deliberately concealed. They might have been inside already and stolen artifacts.

"I have calls to make," he said and reached for the phone.

Braden entered his office the next morning. He closed the door behind him and flipped on the "In Conference. Please do not disturb" light on the door frame. Sitting down behind the desk, he opened the report he'd received from Brent Matthews. He began to read. The bodies of St. Paul and Dumont had been found buried in shallow graves in the woods near the campfires. The search teams determined the officers had been killed by the easternmost fire and dragged into the woods. The rain made their work much more difficult, but they did find ten fired 9mm cartridges close to seven separate bloodstains. Their pistols had not been located. Ballistics testing would determine if the officers' weapons had been fired. The firing pin marks would be compared to samples in Bastogne.

DNA tests proved two of the bloodstains were St. Paul's and Dumont's. As for the other five, the Global DNALINK System would ID them in a few hours. Then they'd know who had also been wounded or killed that night. The bodies had been taken to the Bastogne State Medical Examiner. Preliminary examination showed both died from deep penetrating trauma.

"Stab wounds," Braden muttered to himself. "Shit. Just what I need." He continued reading. With every word his frown deepened. This was disturbing and it directly concerned him. His current caseload included an American Army corporal named Maxwell Hodges, who was being sought for the stabbing murder of a Brussels traffic cop. Braden opened his file drawer and extracted the folder on Hodges. At 1340 hours on the previous Tuesday, Hodges had been stopped for an illegal turn in a Brussels suburb by Officer Jules Leval. Hodges had been told to exit his green 2012 Citroën while Leval wrote out the ticket. Witnesses said the driver, who wore a U.S. Army Class A uniform, had reached into the car and retrieved a long-bladed knife and assaulted Leval by stabbing him multiple times in the belly. Then he got back into the car and drove away, leaving Leval bleeding on the roadside with the knife still in his body.

Leval later died from his wounds in a Brussels emergency room. Hodges's Belgian driver's license and military identification card were left at the scene. The Army's CID was already on the case, but Braden's diplomatic credentials were needed to steer through the maze of foreign law enforcement jurisdictions.

He flipped through the pages, finding Hodges's personnel file. Hodges had been demoted from staff sergeant and was known to be hot-tempered. In the last year, he'd been jailed for drug use, possession, and assault and battery. The Provost Marshal had already begun the process of giving him a dishonorable discharge.

Murder was a capital crime in Belgium, and Hodges, wherever he was, probably knew it. He hadn't crossed the border. The Citroën had been found abandoned on a country road south of the city with an empty tank. His picture had been sent to every bus, rail, air, and maritime port terminal in the country. He wouldn't get far without identification or a car. He had to be desperate.

Braden realized these particular details didn't automatically make Hodges a suspect in the murders of St. Paul and Dumont. But there was one thing that put the army corporal on the list of potential suspects.

He liked edged weapons. Appended to Hodges's file was a report from the Provost Marshal's office at the installation where Hodges was stationed. Hodges had spent much of his pay collecting knives, daggers, stilettos, cutlasses, rapiers, broadswords, cavalry sabers, and bayonets. As per regulations, he'd registered each purchase with the Provost Marshal. The knife Hodges had used to kill Leval was a large French bayonet from the First World War.

Braden leaned back in his chair and closed his eyes. St. Paul and Dumont had been killed by deep penetration wounds from a large knife or sword. If Hodges had been in the forest that night, he was not alone. And if two state police officers had confronted Hodges, he would very likely have reacted violently. It bore some looking into. He checked his E-Rolodex for the number of the Belgian Police Medical Examiner's office in Bastogne. Dr. Hugo Montrose, he read, recalling the name from a previous case. He punched in the number and waited.

"Kortrijk Gemeentepolitie, West Provincie," said the crisp female voice on the phone.

Braden replied in Flemish. "Hello, my name is Alex Braden. I'm an investigator for the NATO Legal Services Department. I would like to speak to Doctor Montrose of the state medical examiner's office, please."

The operator replied in English. "Certainly. Please hold."

A moment later the line was picked up. "This is Doctor Montrose. It's good to hear from you again, Mister Braden. How are you?" His English was perfect.

"I'm well, Doctor, thank you. I'm flattered you remember me."

"I remember good investigators. Now, what can I do for you?"

Braden remembered the last time he'd met Montrose six months ago. He was a slender man, tall and imposing in his neat white lab coat. "You did the postmortem of officers Herbert St. Paul and Henrí Dumont?"

"Yes, why do you ask?"

"I have a case involving an American Army corporal who is being sought for the stabbing murder of a Brussels policeman last Tuesday afternoon. I think there might be a connection. The suspect has a hobby of collecting military and antique edged weapons. When I heard the officers had died of deep penetrating wounds, I decided it bore looking into."

"So you suspect this American soldier to be the killer of St. Paul and Dumont?"

Braden's reply was cautious. "Well, let's just say I'm taking two threads to see if they end up on the same spool."

"Very well, Mister Braden. I will be happy to help. Would you like me to email you the autopsy report?"

"Yes, Doctor. I would appreciate it. You still have my address?" He heard the tapping of a keyboard.

"It's on the way. Do you want to call me back when you've reviewed it?"

Braden thought a moment. "I don't want to take up too much of your time, but would you mind going over the basics of your findings?"

"No problem. Let me open the file."

Braden saw a red light blinking on his phone, but he ignored it. "Thank you. If it seems the soldier might be responsible, I'll contact your investigating officers and send them everything I have. Fair enough?"

Montrose was familiar enough with American idioms to reply in kind. "Fair enough."

Braden accessed his email and found the message from Montrose. After printing the autopsy report, he picked up a pen to make notes.

Montrose cleared his throat. "The time of death for the officers is almost impossible to determine due to the manner of their burial, but forensic evidence shows they were probably killed before 0430 on the morning of their disappearance."

"How was that determined?"

"The storm hit that area around 0445. The soil under the bodies in the shallow graves was still mostly dry."

"Ah. I see. When they were buried, the rain hadn't started. Please continue."

"Patrolman Henrí Dumont, white male, twenty-five years of age, in fit and healthy condition, was killed by two deep penetrating wounds of his upper body. The first wound he received was a straight penetration which entered downward at a shallow angle into his upper-right thorax approximately three centimeters above his right nipple, through the right lung, and exiting from one centimeter to the left edge of his right scapula, the shoulder blade. The weapon used was a long narrow shaft, 1.1 centimeters in diameter with a sharp barb at the end, which was 1.5 centimeters in breadth."

Braden flipped through the printed autopsy report until he found the pertinent page. He frowned. "That sounds like an arrow. But a centimeter thick? That's unusual."

"That's a fair assumption," Montrose agreed. "It was evidently loosed from some distance away since it penetrated downward at an angle of about eighty-five degrees from point of entry. Dumont's second wound was from close range, a deep penetration of his thorax under the sternum by a large bladed weapon. I estimated it to be 4.1 centimeters in breadth."

That was more like it, Braden thought, writing furiously.

Montrose continued. "The wound was thrust up from just under the eleventh rib on the left side, which seems to indicate a right-handed killer stood in front of Dumont."

Hodges was right-handed, but so was eighty percent of the world's population.

"The weapon penetrated the pericardium and the heart," Montrose said, "then the blade was sliced across the abdomen. From right to left, from the killer's point of view, and stopped at the other side of the rib cage."

"Ouch. What a way to die. Sounds almost like seppuku," Braden commented, referring to the Japanese form of ritualistic suicide more commonly known to the west as hara-kiri.

"Yes, it does seem so," Montrose said. "The blade was extremely sharp. The point was in the heart at the apex of a triangle-shaped cut. Dumont was sliced open with great force and a great deal of viciousness."

"As if the killer was angry." Braden thought of Hodges's temper.

"The cut was meant to be fatal. Dumont was alive at that point. He had to have known it was happening."

Hodges had stabbed Leval upward into the body in nearly the same way. "How were you able to determine the sequence of the wounds? That the arrow was first, I mean."

"The sword cut was stopped by the arrow shaft. Also, the man with the sword would have been standing between Dumont and the archer."

More than one killer. Shit. "Can you give me the dimensions of the blade? I need to compare it with those in the soldier's collection."

"Of course. It was about forty centimeters in length and 4.1 in width, straight, with sharp parallel edges. The tapered point was 10.3 centimeters long. The blade was diamond-shaped in cross-section, thicker in the center."

Braden was writing fast. "How could you determine the full length of the blade?"

"Assuming an average-sized man indicates that the grip was about fifteen to twenty centimeters below the lowest part of the blade that touched Dumont's body."

Braden nodded absently, still writing. Too broad for a bayonet.

"If the angle had been different," the doctor said, "I might have considered an old medieval broadsword. It was that heavy."

Braden mulled this over. "Hmm. That's interesting." He quickly sketched what he thought the blade looked like. He frowned. It seemed familiar, but he could not place it. An examination of Hodges's collection might shed some light on it. He returned his attention to the phone. He noticed his message light was blinking. "Is there anything else pertaining to Dumont?"

"Nothing that you'd be interested in, blood analysis, metallurgy."

"Okay. Now on to St. Paul."

"Sergeant Herbert St. Paul. White male, forty years old. Ex-soldier with an excellent record. One old wound; a grazing bullet on the right thigh from his first year on the police force. Good health, though he might have lost a few kilograms. He suffered two wounds, each of which would have been fatal. They were apparently made by the same type of weapons as Dumont's first one. From two arrows."

"No stabbing or slashing wounds?" Braden asked.

"No. Both occurred within seconds of one another and from different angles."

Braden frowned. "I don't understand."

"The first entered his abdomen under the center of his left clavicle, the collarbone, and slid inward at a steep angle, penetrating through his left lung to exit from just to the left of his seventh thoracic vertebrae."

"So it came in from a high angle," Braden concluded.

"Yes," Montrose said. "Very high. At first, we assumed St. Paul might have been on his knees, but there was no indication of this since his trouser legs don't show any sign of being forced against the soil."

"And the second arrow?"

"It entered almost dead-center in the stomach at about eighty degrees, far flatter. It had to be loosed from a very strong bow because it broke the first lumbar vertebrae, splitting it into eleven pieces."

Braden considered this. "Arrows are flimsy objects. I can't imagine an arrow striking bone without breaking. Did you find any fragments from the arrowhead?"

"None. We are looking for traces of metal on the bone fragments. We did find traces of iron oxide and riverbed silt in one of St. Paul's wounds."

"Riverbed silt?" Braden asked, not certain if he had heard correctly.

"Yes. We're having samples of silt from nearby rivers brought for comparison."

"Rust and river mud." Braden rubbed his eyes. "This is getting more bizarre by the minute."

"I agree, but I'm sure of my findings."

Braden had a thought. "Since the arrows came in from different angles and directions, that probably means more than one archer."

Montrose sighed. "It isn't definitive, but I would tend to agree with you on that point, not to make a pun."

Braden smiled. "When the second arrow hit the backbone, he'd have gone down immediately, right?"

"Of course. It would have been like turning off a switch to his legs. The spinal cord was partially severed."

"Would he have been able to shoot accurately?"

Montrose said, "No. The pain would have been excruciating. He must have shot his weapon before being hit."

"Could you determine who died first?"

"St. Paul was killed after Dumont. The crime scene investigators concluded that Dumont and St. Paul had been standing less than three meters apart when they were attacked. When Dumont was hit with the arrow, blood from the exit wound spattered St. Paul's right arm."

I should have known it wouldn't be so cut-and-dried, Braden thought to himself, shaking his head as he looked over three pages of notes. Arrows, for God's sake. "By the way, how were the arrows removed?"

"The shafts were pulled out the way they went in, with a perpetrator placing his foot on Dumont's and St. Paul's chests and yanking them out. The barbs tore at the tissues and skin upon removal."

Braden's forehead furrowed. That didn't make sense. The correct way to remove an arrow from a body was to push it through in the same direction it had entered, thus sliding it out easily. But to yank it out by force the "back way?" That was not only illogical but difficult. And horribly painful if the victim was still alive. It had to be a terrible thing to feel, he thought with a chill. "How did you determine someone had placed their foot on the body?"

"Footprints on the uniform jackets," the medical examiner replied.

Braden glanced at the report but found nothing on the footprints. Hodges had been wearing his Class A uniform shoes when he'd killed Leval. "Did forensics determine the kind of boot or shoe?"

"In a manner of speaking," Montrose said. "I was the first to notice it, but I can tell you it was not a normal boot or shoe. It bore what appeared to be hobnails."

"Hobnails? I thought they'd gone out with Nazi Stormtroopers."

"They still turn up occasionally," Montrose interjected. "I should add that the pattern was irregular as if they were hammered in by hand rather than machine."

Braden shook his head. First arrows, then hobnails. What next?

Montrose interrupted his thoughts. "Do you think your suspect may be involved?" The doctor was being polite but seemed to be nudging Braden into finishing the call.

"Actually, Doctor, I can't see how he could be. If he'd been there and had stabbed Dumont, he'd probably have been shot by St. Paul. We'd know it by now since his DNA is on record. The original reports said that there had been a large number of armed men in the forest. I thought one of them, whoever the others were, might have been our man. Now I'm not so sure. It's as strange a case as any I've ever heard of. But I am very grateful for your time and effort, Doctor. If I come up with anything on our end, I'll be very happy to pass it on."

Montrose was as congenial as ever. "I'm happy to have been of service. I wish you a good day."

"And you too, Doctor."

Braden hung up and sat there with his brow creased in consternation. He didn't know if Corporal Maxwell Hodges had been involved in the murders of St. Paul and Dumont, but an examination of his weapons collection would be the next step. Turning to his computer, he composed an email to his Army CID liaison who was heading up the army's part of the investigation. While Braden was the lead investigator, he always kept CID apprised of progress. After attaching the autopsy report and his notes, he stood up to head out for lunch. Just then, there was a strident knock on his door.

"Crap. Almost made it." He sighed and unlocked the door.

Barney Rabble poked his blond head in. "Don't you ever check your messages?"

Braden suddenly remembered the call he'd ignored while talking to Montrose. He smiled sheepishly. "Sorry, Barn. Just busy."

"Okay, but wait till you see what I have."

"Good news, I hope," Braden said and sat down in his chair.

"Brent heard you were trying to find out if Maxwell Hodges was a suspect in the killings. He came by with this report and saw your 'Go Away and Leave Me the Hell Alone' light on."

Braden grinned.

Rabble continued. "I was coming down the hall, and he gave me this report. He said I might find it interesting and asked if I could give it to you. He had to leave for a deposition."

"Uh-huh." Braden waited.

Rabble smiled again. "I looked it over. I sure did find it interesting. Check it out." He handed Braden a single page.

At the top was the letterhead of the Belgian State Police Forensic Homicide Division.

Blood analysis report
DNALINK TRACE
Case No. 2021-8-79h

87-66
Continued from Page 2
Sample 3: O+ 4654.22220 PR. 00.00 TG. 00.00 ID# UNKNOWN
Sample 4: O+ 4654.10215 PR. 00.00 TG. 00.00 ID# UNKNOWN
Sample 5: A- 4654.54987 PR. 00.00 TG. 00.00 ID# UNKNOWN
Sample 6: AB+ 4564.67844 PR. 00.00 TG. 00.00 ID# UNKNOWN
Sample 7: OB- 4564.84807 PR. 00.00 TG. 00.00 ID# UNKNOWN

Braden finished reading. "Okay, it's a blood report. What does it mean?" He was too tired from his hard morning's work to put up with Rabble's theatrics.

Rabble smirked. "Okay, Al. I'll give you a break. It's the last page from their report about the bloodstains found at the murder scene. Seven separate bloodstains. Two were positively ID'd as St. Paul and Dumont."

"No surprises there," Braden said. "Go on."

"You know they can easily do a DNA trace on blood. Once they have blood, the perp is ID'd by the Global DNALINK System."

Braden sighed. He knew this, as did every competent investigator, police officer, doctor, lab technician, and cop show screenwriter in the world.

Since 2014 all adults, children, even newborns, had been part of an ongoing international cooperative effort to establish a global DNA database. Sponsored by the United Nations, World Health Organization, and the Centers for Disease Control and Prevention, almost 96.1 percent of the world's population, even indigenous tribes, had been entered into a massive database. Its supercomputers could identify DNA samples within minutes via one of six DNALINK centers in Manchester, Washington DC, Johannesburg, Tokyo, Moscow, and Buenos Aires. Once a sample of blood or tissue had been obtained from a crime scene or an unidentified body, it was only a matter of time before the person was identified with a .000000003 percent chance of failure. Three in a billion.

"I seem to recall something about that," Braden said dryly. "I do have a degree in criminal investigation, Barn. So who were they?"

Rabble waited a second before replying. "You'll never guess."

Braden glowered at his visitor. "Okay, I give up. I'll never guess. Who?"

A shrug. "Nobody knows. Five blood samples. Five unknowns."

That almost made Braden's mouth fall open. "What? All five? That's totally impossible."

"Apparently not," said Rabble, clearly pleased with Braden's reaction.

"None came through?"

"Not a one. All were total unknowns. Everyone came up dry, Bundeskriminalamt, French Nationale, Scotland Yard, INTERPOL,

FBI, CIA, Russian RVS, CID, and a ton of other acronyms. All of them are stumped. DNALINK ran it three times and then did it manually. No soap."

Braden looked at the page again. "Damn," he said. "How could that be possible?" DNA tagging was foolproof. The remote possibility that one person might not be in the database was certainly conceivable. But five? The five bloodstains at the crime scene, all ostensibly persons shot by Dumont and St. Paul, were totally unknown to the international DNA database.

Across the desk, Rabble was smiling.

Braden knew him too well. "Barn, you've got more, don't you?"

"Yes, I do. And this one is even better."

Braden sighed as he looked at the ceiling. "Barn, just tell me."

"All right, you know the DNA can be used to find living family members. In the case of an unknown murder victim, even one from long ago, they can find living relatives to aid in the identification."

"Uh-huh."

"The Army is using it to clear up that mess at Arlington Cemetery when they found that hundreds of Civil War graves had been mismarked."

Braden shot him a hard look. "Get to the point, Barn."

Rabble was not to be rushed. "They can also tell with reasonable accuracy how many generations there are between two related samples. In the case of someone dead a hundred years, it should be no more than three or four generations."

"A generation being what?" Braden asked. "Twenty or twenty-five years?"

"Close enough," Rabble said.

"Go on." Braden was watching his friend carefully. This had to be big the way Rabble was toying with him.

"Those samples were run through the system to find any living relatives to aid in identification with a probable generation count thrown in for good measure."

"Hold on," Braden interrupted, "those men were alive up to two days ago. Even if they were old, like in their eighties, it couldn't be more than two generations. Why are you bringing that up?"

Rabble grinned again. "Wrong, my friend. They did find ninety-three persons, mostly of Mediterranean extraction, who come from the same family line as three of the unknowns."

Braden leaned forward in his chair. "That many? Great. We might have a break there." The smug expression on Rabble's face made him cringe.

Rabble also leaned closer. "Nope. They never met these men. You see, they are at least seventy-five to eighty generations removed from the men whose blood was found." He sat back, still grinning.

Braden heard the words but couldn't grasp their meaning. "How many?"

"Seventy-five to eighty," Rabble repeated. "They ran the test three times with careful checks to make sure the samples hadn't been degraded. They were clean. No doubt. The DNALINK lab technicians were flummoxed, as you'd expect."

"So there has to be a mistake somewhere."

"Nope. Remember, they did find living descendants. Italian, mostly. A few Turks, French, Greek, and Spanish."

Braden's eyes were wide. "Seventy-five to eighty generations, that's about . . . uh . . ." He tried the mental math, but Rabble beat him to it.

"About two thousand years, give or take a century."

CHAPTER X

BREAKING NEWS

Stefan Barat had been able to keep his secret for exactly four days. Sure, he'd bragged about screwing Charlotte. That hadn't been much of a secret. But the midnight rides into the woods were. Stefan's best friend Jules Collet had prodded him for details. Jules was still a virgin, a source of never-ending shame for the seventeen-year-old.

Stefan and Jules were lounging on their motorcycles in the high school car park when a girl their age passed by, winking at Stefan. She was pretty and slim with long, straight auburn hair.

"God," Jules moaned, sipping a soda. "I would love to have that."

Stefan grinned. "It's not that hard. She is easy. All you have to do is get her drunk."

"Sure, that's all there is to it," his friend remarked sarcastically. "She won't even look at me."

"If you weren't so ugly, she might," Stefan poked at him.

Stefan genuinely liked Jules, but the guy didn't have any guts. He was afraid to try anything.

Jules sighed. "How do you get Charlotte to let you do her?"

Stefan shrugged. "She's willing. I can get her anytime."

"Monsieur Renaud would shoot you if he caught you together."

"We have ways," Stefan said cryptically. "I meet her at night. After her parents are in bed."

Jules snorted. "And you just go and fuck her in her bed?"

Stefan rolled his eyes. "Of course not. We go out into the country. She likes to do it under the stars."

"Wow. How often?"

"Used to be about twice a week."

"And now?" Jules asked, keen to know the details.

"She won't go out right now," Stefan admitted. Every attempt he'd made to get her to go out again had met with lame excuses.

"Why not?"

"Oh, last week we were doing it in a valley north of her father's farm, and something happened that scared her."

"She saw your face?" Jules thought that was funny.

Stefan hit him on the arm. "No, you idiot. We saw some men marching in the night."

"Who? Army soldiers on maneuvers?" Jules's father was in the army.

Stefan thought for a moment. He was sworn to secrecy, but if he couldn't tell his best friend . . . "Well, no. They weren't soldiers. Do you remember last year when we went to that renaissance fair near Épernay?"

"Sure. My father took us. He told us all about the medieval wars and stuff."

"Yeah," Stefan said. "But there were some other groups there. And they were like Romans or something."

"Oh, those guys," Jules said, nodding. "A Roman legion. Remember they did that battle? That was cool."

"Those are the ones," Stefan said. "They wore red skirts and armor and carried shields."

"Uh-huh." Jules was looking at him quizzically. "What about it?"

"I'd just fucked her, and we were lying back when the ground started to shake. Charlotte freaked and we moved into the trees. A minute later, here comes this whole army of Romans or something. All in armor and helmets and spears and stuff. Maybe a thousand of them."

"This was at night?" Jules asked with wide eyes.

"About two in the morning."

"Cool!" Jules said. "I wonder what a reenactment group would be doing out there in the middle of the night."

Stefan bit his lip. "I don't think they were reenactors."

"What else could they be?"

Stefan shrugged. "Well . . . They were really dirty and unshaven. Sort of like your father looks after a week of maneuvers. They weren't neat and polished like the ones we saw at the fair. They looked dangerous, I guess." He stopped. "Listen, don't tell anyone, okay? Charlotte would kill me if she knew I told you. She's scared her father will find out."

"Okay," Jules said. He stood and checked his watch. "I gotta go and do some chores before supper." Then he looked at his friend. "Anyway, it's not like it was anything real. They had to be reenactors."

Stefan sighed. "I guess." No way in hell.

That evening at dinner, Jules let his talk with Stefan slip to his father, a sergeant in the French Army. Sergeant Louis Collet had been in command of a squad of anti-terrorist troops two years before, and anything involving armed men piqued his interest. The older man questioned his son further. Collet decided to have a talk with Stefan himself.

The sound of his bedside phone ringing intruded into Braden's dream. He squinted in the dark. Without turning on the light, he reached for the phone. "Yes?" He tried not to sound annoyed.

"Hey, love. Did I wake you?" Ann's velvet voice slid into his ears like cream into tea. He smiled. "Yes, but that's okay." He looked to see the glowing red digital numbers on his clock. It read 12:55. "Why are you calling me this late? I have to go to work tomorrow. Today," he corrected himself.

"Sorry, love," came her reply. "I just had to ring you up. You've got to see this."

"See what?" Braden wasn't fully awake.

"Turn on the telly, you sleepy bugger," she said insistently. "Euro Network News. Right now. They'll repeat it in a moment, I think."

"All right, all right." He reached past the phone to pick up the remote. He yawned, not bothering to stifle it.

Ann didn't take the bait. "Got it on yet?"

He rubbed his eyes. "ENN. Okay, got it. A report on . . . what? A bear that got loose in London Zoo? Why in the hell would I be interested in that?"

"Not the bloody bear," Ann said. "Hang in there. They're bound to repeat it quickly. It's the top story. So how're things at the office?"

The non sequitur caught him off guard and Braden mumbled, "I'm working on a very strange case."

"I'm sorry I woke you, but I just know you're going to be thrilled by what's happening in France."

"France?" Braden mumbled.

"Here it is! Now watch!"

He turned up the volume. The ENN anchorperson, a lovely woman with short black hair, was talking in French. "—an incredible discovery in the Champagne region of France which archaeologists and historians are already calling one of the most stunning historical finds in over a century." The inset video was panning over a grassy slope illuminated from banks of bright floodlights. Yellow CAUTION tape was erected around the perimeter of a large black pit in the hillside. Braden saw men and women wearing miner's helmets emerging from it. "The entrance to what appears to be an unknown Roman cellar, one of the few ever found in the region, was discovered by vintner André Robert. So far, the full extent of the cellar has not been explored due to its immense size, but early reports state that it seems to hold an unbelievable wealth of artifacts and possibly even human remains."

"Holy shit!" Braden exclaimed.

"Thought you'd say that, love," was Ann's satisfied reply. "You're on your own. Have fun. Love you."

"I love you too," he replied. "By the way, what were you doing up so early?"

"Late. I've been reading a wonderful new Mark Carlson novel I couldn't put down. And before I put myself in for the night, I turned on ENN, and there it was. Quite a find, eh?"

"Sure seems to be. Okay, you get to bed, honey. I'll call you later."

Ann laughed. "Not too early. I have to fly to Edinburgh at noon. I'm going to sleep in."

Braden didn't reply to the irony. He made a kissing sound and hung up. The reporter, a clean-cut man of thirty with windblown light brown hair and hazel eyes, faced the camera. "This is Jason Cannell at the Robert Winery outside Reims. We're talking with Professor Arthur Morley of Cambridge University, who has been examining this extraordinary find." The camera turned toward a sixtyish-year-old man wearing a yellow miner's helmet.

Cannell held the microphone close to Morley. "Professor, what can you tell us about this discovery?"

"Well," Morley began in a smooth, cultured English accent, "it is undoubtedly the largest cellar of its kind ever found in the region. Further exploration of the site will reveal more information, but a final assessment is months, possibly years off, due to the extent of the find."

He took off the helmet. Arthur Morley had wavy gray hair above thick black eyebrows. A pair of gold-rimmed glasses was perched on the end of his long nose. Braden remembered Morley's name from his reading. Professor of Classical European Archaeology Arthur Morley was a historian of impeccable reputation who had written several books on Ancient Rome.

The reporter asked, "Do you have any idea how far it extends?"

Morley shook his head. "Not yet. A preliminary survey has revealed a long central hallway well over a hundred meters in length and fifteen rooms on either side. There is a huge storeroom at the far end, but due to poor ventilation, we haven't yet explored it. We hope to have the proper equipment here in a few hours."

"Can you confirm if it is indeed a Roman cellar?" Cannell asked.

"It appears to be. Other Roman cellars have much the same general construction, but this one is far greater in scope and complexity."

"Have any artifacts been found and identified?"

"Yes," Morley said, adjusting his glasses. "A wealth of preserved Roman-era personal gear has been found, as well as garments, armor, and weapons. They appear to date to the early first century. It's all quite remarkable." He smiled warmly. "Now, if you'll excuse me, I really must get back to my work."

"Thank you for your time, Professor Morley," the reporter said. He turned back to the camera. "At the Robert Vineyards archaeological site, this is Jason Cannell, Euro Network News. Back to you, Nicholette."

The woman's face again filled the screen. "Thank you, Jason. ENN will be bringing you further coverage of the find in Champagne, France, of an unknown Roman cellar as events break. In Berlin, Chancellor Hoffman's cabinet—"

Braden muted the TV, not interested in news he probably knew better than ENN did, and sat in the dark, letting what he'd just learned wash over him. "Wow," he said aloud. "What a find. That will be a real bonanza for history." He glanced at the clock. It read 1:22. After turning off the television, he crawled back under the covers and tried to sleep.

But his mind was racing with what Morley had said. They'd found weapons. Roman weapons. Why did that seem important?

Finally, Braden's mind slowed down and he drifted off.

CHAPTER XI

THE MARCH AGAINST TIME

The next day Jules and his father found Stefan working at the bike shop.

"Stefan, I want to know what you and that girl saw that night in the woods."

Stefan shot Jules a dirty look but quailed under the sergeant's hard gaze. "Yes, sir." He described what he'd seen.

"They had weapons?" Collet asked him.

Stefan nodded enthusiastically. "Lots of them, spears and swords and stuff."

"No guns?" Collet jotted down some notes.

"None that I could see. Just swords and stuff. And shields. I couldn't tell what color, but they had some sort of wings on them."

The sergeant looked at him. "Painted on, you mean?"

"Yeah." Stefan saw that some girls from the ice cream shop next door were listening in. He was starting to enjoy being so important.

"You said there were a thousand of them?" Collet frowned. "Are you sure you're not exaggerating?"

"No," Stefan said, shaking his head. "There were so many that it took about twenty minutes for all of them to pass."

"They didn't see you?" Collet prompted. He really didn't care the teens had been screwing in the woods. Kids did things like that. But armed men creeping in the night was another matter.

"No. They kept marching and that was all."

"I see," Collet said, looking over his notes. "Is there anything else?"

Stefan smiled at the girls. "Oh yeah, they had scouts out front away from the rest. With long spears. Sort of looking around."

"That's interesting," Collet said, writing. "I want to know exactly where this happened."

Stefan told the sergeant where he and Charlotte had seen the strange soldiers.

Collet slipped his notepad into a pocket. "Okay, Stefan. I don't know if this is important, but I thank you for your help."

After Jules and his father left, Stefan was suddenly the center of attention. He told the story to the attentive girls. What was the point of being quiet now? Charlotte would be angry, but the other girls would want to know more. He'd take them into the forest at night, too.

Lucius led his legion down the valley of the Moselle River. The wide Rhenus, the border between Belgicae and Germania, was less than a night's march away. Three days and nights had passed since the fight with the two intruders. Five legionaries had been killed with the strange noisy weapons. Lucius had been angered, not only for the loss of good men but because he wanted to learn more from the intruders.

They were taken away and buried in shallow graves as it started to drizzle. The five legionaries were taken even farther away to be buried. Lucius intended to delay detection as long as possible. But time was running out, and he knew it.

Septimus kept the "fire hammers" for study. The talking thing had not spoken again. He had asked it questions, but it said nothing to him. "Perhaps the spirit inside would only speak to one of the dead men."

The rain started in earnest as they gathered their gear and the remaining meat and marched east. Their footprints soon disappeared in the pelting downpour. Lucius wanted to put as much distance between themselves and the place in the event anyone came looking for the two men. They crested a hill where a wide road ran across their path. The rain cut down visibility, but the glowing lamps on the metal chariots were easy to see from a distance. They crossed the road and disappeared into the dense forest. Lucius told Plutonius to watch for the headwaters of the Sauer River and follow it to the southeast.

Lucius's mind was in turmoil. How could it be? He had physically staggered upon reading the numbers on the paper. MMDCCLXXIV. Two thousand years! It was not possible. But, he had to admit to himself, it explained so much. The world had changed. Everything was faster, louder, bigger, brighter, and more dangerous. There was no one in Rome who would remember him. Augustus, that great but damaged leader, was no more. Even Rome itself might have crumbled into the dust of the ages. Lucius kept these thoughts to himself, knowing that every man in Legio LIV was thinking exactly the same things.

The men talked little while they marched east in the rain. They crossed roads and followed a swollen stream, keeping in the heaviest part of the woods along the banks.

At one point, Plutonius climbed a ridge that sloped southeast and reported the bright glow of a city to the south. "It was many miles distant," he said to Lucius upon returning. "The rain and mist made it difficult to see clearly, but it was a large city. I saw the lights of some smaller villages to the north as well."

"Which direction should we follow?" Lucius asked.

Plutonius pointed eastward. "If we stay in the valley of this river, we will stay clear of any towns. I only saw isolated lights. We will meet up with the Moselle tomorrow."

Lucius nodded. "Very well. Continue the march at once."

The following night they had approached the largest road they'd ever seen. It was a vast expanse that stretched out of sight past the wooded hills to the north and south. The rain turned the surface into a polished onyx mirror in the glare of the metal chariots' lights. The road crossed over the rain-swollen river. Keeping to the muddy banks, the legionaries were able to pass under the bridge without being seen by the vehicles.

"Fascinating," Septimus said, admiring the smooth concrete span over them. "The advances in construction are astounding. The concrete is so smooth."

In a short time, the legion was past the road and moving east in the dark woods. When dawn rose, they found a deep hollow in the woods that served for cover during the day. The rain came and went, and Lucius was certain that no one would be around. He told his men to sleep.

On the next night, the rain slackened and stopped. The wet and bedraggled legionaries wrung out their blankets to dry off while on the move. By then, the meat had been consumed and digested. The steady march on a diet of grapes, berries, vegetables, and fruit while fighting off cold and damp was fast draining them of their stamina.

Lucius saw several legionaries weaving with fatigue. "We cannot go on as we are," he said to Marcus and Vitellus. "We need more meat. Tell Plutonius to alert us to the next farm with livestock."

Within an hour the scouts found a large farm with pigs and cattle. Lucius hadn't wanted to risk the theft of animals, but he was convinced by his own increasing hunger. Vitellus led twenty men out of the woods and across a road to a large enclosure that held at least a hundred sleeping pigs. He kept a wary eye on the dark farmhouse. They climbed into the nearest pen, feeling the dank evil-smelling mud squelch around their feet. Vitellus's nose crinkled as he drew his knife. He approached a large pig and drove the blade into the animal's neck just behind the head. The spine was instantly severed, and the pig died without a sound. "That is what you must do," he whispered. "Right there. We cannot make any noise."

Three more pigs were quietly dispatched. Then one man lost his footing in the mud and fell onto the pig he had been approaching. The pig grunted and squealed loudly, rising to its feet. The legionary reacted quickly by slashing out and cutting the animal's throat. A loud gurgle and more squeals erupted from the pig. Several others grunted; then it was over. Silence again came over the night, and no light came on in the house. They dragged the dead pigs out of the pen and back to the safety of the forest.

"How many?" Lucius asked when the hunters returned.

"Five, Sire," Vitellus replied. "Plenty for a few days."

"Well done, Marius Vitellus. Sling them from poles. We need to put distance between us and here."

Septimus, who had been taking a muster of the legion, informed Lucius that since leaving the cellar, the death toll was 134. Just under nine hundred men were left.

Will we make it? Lucius wondered. *So far to go, so few left.*

Braden was reading over the Provost Marshal's report on Hodges's weapons collection when Rabble entered without knocking at a quarter after nine.

"Something strange has been happening in France and Belgium," Rabble said.

Braden looked up with a puzzled expression. "What do you mean by strange?"

Rabble sat down across from him. "Katy Williams down in communications has been busy. Yesterday I asked her to give me anything odd that came in on the Internet. And boy did she deliver." He held up a sheaf of printed pages. "Last Friday night, two French kids screwing in the woods saw a strange armored army marching east in the night. They kept it quiet until yesterday. A French Army sergeant sent in the report."

Braden nodded. The best means to advance an investigation was open communication. Rabble was the best intuitive investigator at NATO. "Go on."

"On Sunday morning, a number of passengers on a tourist train saw at least three men wearing gray cloaks, red skirts, and armor and carrying big shields and spears standing at the edge of the woods. It was one of those antique steam excursion trains. A lot of passengers thought the men were part of the tour, but when they asked the conductors about it, they were clueless."

"Any pictures?"

Rabble shook his head. "No, I guess it was too fast and no one was ready. But at least twenty people saw them."

Braden was listening closely now, even though he had no idea where Rabble was going with this.

Rabble flipped to the next page. "Then, a French forest gardien, what we would call a ranger, driving his patrol bike near the west bank of the Meuse River, found signs of a big campsite in the woods. It was apparent a large number of people had stayed the night." He paused. "That was less than five hundred meters from where the train had gone by."

It was obvious to Braden that Rabble had done some investigating.

"Next," Rabble continued, "the murders of St. Paul and Dumont, fifteen klicks east of the Meuse River, east of the border and deep in the Ardennes." He paused. "Almost directly on the other side of the river from the campsite and train sighting."

Braden whistled. "You're kidding."

Rabble shook his head. "Nope. And here's the best one. This morning, a Belgian rancher reported five of his hogs missing and found bloodstains in the mud. He saw trails of footprints and drag marks leading from the pen to the road. Whoever did it had probably driven off." Rabble leaned back in the chair. "A lot of weird things. Farmers have been reporting stolen chickens, stripped vegetable patches, and stuff like that. I'm seeing a pattern here."

"Looks that way to me too." Braden turned around in his chair and reached for a large rolled topographical map of Northern Europe. "Let's find out." He unrolled it on his desk and weighted it down with a coffee mug and stapler. "Let's start with the French kids. Where was it?"

Rabble leaned over the map. "Just east of Rethel in this narrow valley here."

"Okay." Braden put a mark on the spot with a pencil. "And the train?"

Rabble pointed to a railroad line on the map. "Here. About twenty klicks farther east. The gardien found the campsite on the west bank of the river."

"Got it." Another two marks were placed on the map.

"St. Paul and Dumont were killed about ten klicks inside the border."

"Right, I have that one," Braden confirmed, putting a fourth mark on the map. "Next?"

"The stolen pigs report was about fifty klicks farther east," Rabble said, checking his notes and pointing. "Right about there."

After putting a final mark on the map, Braden reached into his desk drawer and withdrew a long steel ruler. He placed one end on the location of the stolen livestock and the edge on the place where the French kids had seen the men in the night.

Rabble leaned close. "Shit. They don't line up. Maybe I was wrong."

Braden continued to stare at the map. "Yes, they do, Barn. Just not the way you think. Terrain makes a perfectly straight march impossible. Keeping out of sight and moving around obstacles also causes deviations." He sat down, fiddling with the pencil. "It's interesting that nearly all the incidents took place about twenty or thirty klicks apart. That's how far someone can walk in eight hours. That line is connected by geography and time."

Rabble let out a breath. "Like I said, it's weird. A lot of really unusual things happen in a little under a week. It's probably not a coincidence."

"Hardly," Braden snorted. "But who the hell is it?" He allowed his eyes to roam over to the glass-fronted cabinet containing his artifact collection. Helmets, belt buckles, and insignia were carefully displayed on the shelves. He saw the glint of the small bronze disk on crimson velvet. It triggered a thought. Red skirts. Armor. Romans? "No. It can't be."

"What?" For once, Rabble seemed confused.

Braden shook his head in irritation. "How the hell did I miss it? It was socking me in the face the whole time!" He snatched up the notes he'd made of the autopsy report. A sentence jumped out at him. Forty centimeters in length, four across. Double-edged with straight, parallel sides tapering to a point ten centimeters long. "Oh, my God . . ." His voice trailed off.

"You have something?"

Braden glanced up. "I'm not positive. But these," he tapped the pencil on the page, "are my notes about the autopsies on St. Paul and Dumont. Something just clicked." He handed the pages to his friend.

"Well, don't keep me in suspense," Rabble prompted.

"The sword that killed Dumont was unusual. I don't know why I didn't think of it then, but it perfectly matches the dimensions of a Roman Gladius."

"A what?"

"A Roman sword. About this long," he said, holding his hands about a half meter apart. "The dimensions of the stab wound are right on the money."

Rabble was reading the notes. "Okay. What about the arrows? Did Sioux Indians also attack them?"

Braden shrugged. "The rest of the wounds were made by something like arrows. But I've never heard of arrows that thick or strong." Then he felt his skin go cold. Pilum? "Damn . . . that fits. It actually fits!"

Rabble didn't interrupt.

"No arrow could remain intact after breaking bone." Braden frowned and spoke slowly. "But a pilum could."

"Okay," Rabble said, holding his hands out. "What exactly is a pilum?"

"A spear," Braden responded, reaching back to his bookcase and pulling out a large book. After flipping through the pages, he turned it around and showed it to Rabble. He pointed at a photo. "It's about two meters long with a wood handle attached through a lead weight to a barbed iron shaft. It fits perfectly."

Rabble examined the picture. "Not an arrow?"

"Goddamn," Braden said. "It really fits. A fucking pilum!" His skin was tingling.

"Hold on," Rabble said with a frown. "You're saying someone with Roman weapons killed them?"

"Sure. Why not?" Braden said excitedly. "It'd be impossible to guess unless you're familiar with Roman weapons. Even I missed it. They match perfectly, even in the way they were used. The pilum was thrown overhand to stab down into the enemy, and the gladius was thrust up into the body under the ribs." He made a thrusting motion with the pencil, which looked ludicrous. Then he chuckled. "I know it sounds crazy, but maybe someone is using reproduction weapons to kill. It's a new one, isn't it?"

"Sure is," Rabble agreed.

Then Braden had another thought. "Armored men carrying shields and wearing red skirts. That's what a Roman legionary looks like."

"So a bunch of reenactors went off the deep end?"

Braden was about to speak but then stopped. What *did* he mean? "I don't know, Barn. But people dressed as Romans are out there marching in the night."

Rabble rested his chin on his hand. "Remember those pictures? The ones Brent showed us?"

Braden's head snapped around. "Yeah. We couldn't see any details. But now I think on it, the men in those photos did have the silhouette of Roman legionaries." He banged a fist against his leg. "Why didn't I recognize them? I just saw a huge reenactment on Saturday."

"I'll ask Brent if they were able to enhance them," Rabble said, standing up. He reached for the doorknob.

Then he heard Braden say, "Holy shit!"

Rabble turned. "What?"

Braden was looking at the map. His face suddenly looked ashen. "We left out one thing."

"What's that?" Rabble asked, going back to the desk.

"Right here," Braden said, tapping a finger where the ruler's end was directly over a small valley northeast of Reims. "This is where they found that Roman cellar the other day."

"Oh yeah. I saw that on ENN. But what's that got to do with the murders and the sightings?"

"Don't you see it, Barn? They found a lot of artifacts. Roman armor and clothing. And weapons."

Rabble looked at him quizzically. "You think . . ."

Sliding the Hodges file from under the map, Braden said, "I have to find out if Hodges had ever collected any Roman weapons. Then I may have to go to France."

"To the cellar?" Rabble asked.

"I'm investigating a murder committed last Tuesday in Brussels by a man who likes swords. Two other murders a few days later in the same region were committed using Roman weapons. And now an unknown Roman cellar packed with artifacts turns up? It's one hell of a coincidence, Barn. I have to find out."

CHAPTER XII

INTO THE PIT

The flight from Brussels landed at the Reims airport ten minutes after noon the next day. Braden showed his NATO credentials and passport and breezed through customs. Ten minutes later he was in a blue Peugeot. He programmed the GPS for the Robert Vineyards and headed north. Reims was a fair-sized city for the Champagne region and still held much of its quaint medieval ambiance as a tourist mecca for those interested in French culture, music, food, and wine. Half an hour after leaving the airport, Braden was passing between low rolling green hills dotted with orchards, vineyards, and old country homes. He saw news vans on the side of the winding country road. Slowing to weave carefully among the clusters of people and vehicles, he found a turnoff blocked by a private security guard. The man leaned toward the car window and spoke a question in French.

Braden pulled out his passport and NATO credentials. "I am here to meet Professor Morley."

The guard checked a list and nodded. "I have you on the list, Monsieur Braden. Please continue on this road until you come to the clearing by the vineyard. You can park there." He tossed a respectful salute to the NATO man, who returned it with a smile. Braden drove on, seeing several people walking along the road. It was a busy place. After cresting a hill, he came to a large graveled parking area full of cars and vans. Most bore the emblems of universities and government agencies. He found a space and climbed out, feeling the hot wind on his face. Pulling his shoulder bag from the front seat, he saw a woman standing next to a large van. He trotted over. "Hello, pardon me for interrupting, but I wonder if you could tell me where I could find Professor Morley?"

The woman was pulling a large aluminum case from the van. She replied without looking up. "He's busy right now and can't give any interviews."

"Ah . . . Well, I'm not here for an interview. I have an appointment. I'm with NATO."

She still hadn't turned around. She had red hair in a long single braid down her back, resembling a thick rope of copper. Then she turned and looked up at him. Her eyes were a pale green the color of jade. She was also attractive. "Oh, I'm sorry. I thought you were another reporter." She rolled her eyes. "You wouldn't believe how many have been trying to get to Arthur."

Braden grinned. "No apologies necessary, Miss . . ."

"Doctor Sharon Kelly," she said, holding out her hand. "Forensic archaeologist."

"Glad to meet you, Doctor Kelly. Alex Braden." He took her hand. It was warm and sweaty.

"Sorry," she said again, wiping her hand on her shorts. "Hot out here. Call me Sharon."

"Forensic archaeology," Braden said. "That's fascinating. You must be finding some incredible discoveries in there."

Sharon expelled a long breath. "You have no idea. It's a treasure trove of new information and data on the first-century Roman Army." Sliding the van door closed, she picked up the case and motioned for him to follow. "Arthur's this way." She had a Boston accent.

"You're from New England?"

"Chelsea. Studied anthropology and archaeology at Harvard then got my postgrad degree and doctorate at MIT." She spoke over her shoulder as she walked. She wore a tan work shirt and shorts over sturdy walking shoes.

"Anything in there you can tell me about?"

"Lots. Clothing, artifacts, weapons, armor, foodstuffs, you name it. It'll take years to curate. But the real prize is the bodies."

He stopped, stunned. Then he jogged to catch up with her. "Bodies? Of Roman legionaries? That's unbelievable. How could the remains have survived?"

"That's part of the mystery," Sharon remarked as she turned down a well-trodden path between two vineyards. The tall vines were festooned with bunches of pale-yellow grapes ripening in the sun. "We expected bones, and we found plenty, but there are some that still hold flesh and even hair. It's remarkable. Cloth, leather, lots of organic things are in excellent condition." She stopped beside a large blue open-sided marquee tent. "Here we are." She put the case on a folding table. The marquee tent shaded chairs and more tables that held notebook computers, scanners, and other equipment. "Arthur's over there by the pit. He'll be here in a moment."

Braden looked to where she was pointing. Beyond the tent was a flat area of bare soil ending at the base of a steep brush-covered hillside. A narrow black opening like the entrance to a mine was cut into it. He thought it looked like the doorway to Hell. A large solar-powered generator hummed nearby, its thick cables running down into the open hole. Professor Arthur Morley was speaking to four other people. They were listening to him and typing notes on their iPads. "That'll do for now," he said with a smile. "Off you go." They turned and stepped into the black opening. They seemed to disappear instantly.

"Professor," Sharon said.

Morley looked at her, but his attention seemed to be on something else. "Yes, Sharon?"

"Someone to see you. From NATO."

The old professor's thick eyebrows lifted like black wings. He walked over to Braden and held out his hand. "Ah, Mister Bradley, right?"

"Braden. Alex Braden." They shook hands.

Morley grinned. "I'm quite sorry. I have a lot on my mind. Pleased to meet you, Mister Braden. I'm very grateful you could see me on such short notice." The older man was avuncular and friendly. "Now, what brings a representative of NATO to our humble digs?"

"Actually, it's both business and pleasure, Professor. I have an unusual interest in this matter. I'm investigating some murders in Belgium."

Morley looked surprised. "Murders? Dear me, this might prove to be interesting, to say the least." He motioned for Braden to sit in a canvas director's chair. "Would you like something cold to drink? Ice tea, lemon squash, soft drinks, or water?"

"Please just call me Alex. Lemon, please," he said, sitting down and accepting a cold bottle that Morley retrieved from a large cooler. "Thank you." He noticed Sharon was still nearby, sitting at a folding table examining a bronze bowl. "I'm a criminal investigator and working on two cases that might be connected to your discovery. The main one involves the murder of two Belgian state police officers a few days ago. They were killed by deep penetration wounds that were caused by what appear to be a Roman gladius and at least three pila."

Sharon's head snapped around. Morley sat down in front of Braden. "Is that so? And how did you come to that conclusion?" His tone was not accusatory but curious.

"I've been a student of ancient military history most of my life. I've read all the books I could find on the Roman Army and its weapons. As a matter of fact, I read your book, *The First Conquest,* a couple of years ago." He shook his head. "It took me a long time to connect the pathology of the wounds with the Roman sword and spear, but it fit perfectly." He took a long pull from the bottle. The lemonade was a French brand and quenched his thirst at once.

Morley listened politely with his chin resting on his palm. "Remarkable. Can you show me some evidence of this?"

"Here's the report from the coroner of the Bastogne Police headquarters," Braden replied, sliding a folder out of his bag. He handed it to Morley, who put on a pair of glasses and peered through them. His brows met in the center of a crease over his nose. Sharon moved close and read over his shoulder. He didn't seem to mind. "This is remarkable," he said again. "Simply remarkable."

Braden looked at the black opening in the earth a few meters away, wondering at the incredible things which must be inside. A murmur from Morley made him look back.

"Yes, the wounds are very indicative of the gladius and pilum, as you said." He handed the file to Sharon. "And I agree there is probably no other weapon which fits the bill, so to speak. But what can that have to do with this cellar?"

"On the news broadcast I saw on ENN, you said a great number of weapons had been found in the cellar, which was discovered close to when the policemen were killed. That's a hell of a coincidence, you must admit. I merely decided to see if there was a common thread."

"So you think some of the weapons from the cellar might have been used in the killings?" This was from Sharon.

Braden shrugged. "Who's to say for sure? I don't believe in such coincidences. Do you?"

"I see all kinds in my work, Alex," the old academician smiled. "But I must admit this is intriguing."

Braden leaned forward. "Let me ask you this. Can you ascertain if any weapons are missing?"

Morley and Sharon exchanged significant looks. Braden glanced back and forth between them. "What?"

Sharon smiled. "Sorry. It's just that . . . Well, there are thousands of swords and spears down there. And it might be impossible to say if any had been stolen."

Braden absorbed this. "How many?"

"Enough to arm an entire legion."

"That many?" His eyes were wide.

"Well," Morley cautioned, "most of a legion. Some things don't fit together yet."

"I don't understand."

Morley stood up. "Why don't we take a walk, and I'll show you." He looked down at Braden's shoes. "Those will do," he said. He handed Braden a hardhat and a pair of latex gloves and led the way to the tunnel opening. "You'll need both hands free on the stone stairs."

Sharon was still reading the report and said, "Have a nice time."

Morley and Braden stooped to enter the dark opening. There were rubber mats on the dirt floor and large spotlights illuminating the entire passageway into the depths. Braden couldn't see to the bottom. A stone ramp paralleled the steps to about halfway to the entrance tunnel. A huge stone block, nearly a meter square, rested on the top of the ramp. Next to the ramp was a stack of heavy wooden timbers and metal pry bars. "How deep is it?"

"From the mean surface level to the floor is about twenty-three meters." Morley led the way down the stone steps.

Like most modern Americans, Braden still tended to convert metric numbers. Seventy-five feet. He realized he was about to enter a structure built two thousand years ago. The time of Christ. He felt the air temperature drop noticeably with every few steps they descended.

"When the cellar was discovered by André Robert," Morley said, "he realized it had probably been opened earlier. A great number of footprints had been evident in the area."

The bottom of the stairs came into view. "The boards sealing the entrance were tight and firm. It is possible someone found it but did not open it, choosing instead to come back later." The professor reached the bottom step and moved aside for Braden. "Welcome to the first century."

The simple statement made Braden's skin crawl. What greeted him was a cross between a movie set and a biblical legend. Floodlights and fluorescent bars mounted on wheeled tripods cast bright pools of light into every corner of the long hallway. It stretched off into the distance like a railroad tunnel. It was wide enough for two cars to pass by each other beneath a vaulted ceiling of heavy gray stone. Along both walls were arched doorways.

A dozen people armed with measuring tools, iPads, digital cameras, and other instruments were busily making measurements, taking photos, and recording data. Braden whistled in amazement.

"Do you like our little hole in the ground?" Morley asked, leaning on the wall. "It is quite remarkable, wouldn't you say?"

"That isn't nearly a strong enough word, Professor," Braden said. "I've never seen anything like it. How far does it extend?"

"Two hundred and eighty meters to the far end," Morley answered, motioning for Braden to follow. "There are fifteen doorways on each side.

Sixty rooms in sets of two. They are approximately fifteen meters square and contain bunks and bedding. At the far end is a larger room, over thirty meters square, containing racks of armor and weapons, marching impedimenta, and so on."

Braden looked at the walls. "Was it dug from the hillside?"

Morley shook his head. "We're still trying to determine that. There are many natural limestone caverns in the region. This may have once been a natural cave and expanded. The stone is also common in the area. It must have taken several thousand men at least a year to dig, quarry, and construct the cellar."

Braden slowly nodded. "And other rooms? Like officers' quarters?"

"No," Morley said with a shake of his head. "In fact, there are no other rooms at all that we've discovered. Just barracks. No officers' quarters, no kitchen, no medical rooms, no rooms for livestock, no baths, nothing at all. Not even latrines."

"But all Roman forts and camps had extensive support facilities," Braden pointed out. "Why is this one different?"

"I can't imagine. It's cost me some sleep. I can only assume there must be another cellar. We've had surveyors looking and probing nearby. Nothing."

Braden commented on the chill. "Cold down here."

"About five degrees Celsius. Very dry. It would be perfect for aging wine and spirits."

Peering into the first open doorway, Braden saw the heavy door had a thick leather trim on all four edges. It looked like weather seal or a gasket. "The walls look very thick," he observed.

Morley nodded. "Roman vaulted ceilings required strong support."

There were carved letters in the doorway lintel. Cohor. I Cento. I. "The first century of Cohort Primus?" asked Braden.

"All the lintels have it," Morley said. "The inner room is for the second century."

"Each room quartered a century?"

Morley led the way into the room. "Apparently. The last room on the left is for the sixth century of Cohort Decimus."

The room contained rows of single and three-tiered heavy wooden bunks. At the back was another doorway. On the floor along the walls were dozens of bronze bowls. Each was about the size of a colander and contained a burned substance like charred dust. Braden bent to peer at the nearest one. "What are these? Lanterns?"

Morley shrugged. "We're not sure. Sharon's looking into it. But there are thousands of them."

Braden examined the closest bunk. It was built of heavy dark wood. A layer of gray decayed fabric covered the bed planks. "Were these ever used?"

"Yes. We found hair and wool clothing fibers on all of them. The mattresses were linen, probably stuffed with straw or hemp."

They returned to the main hall. "Sixty rooms," murmured Braden. "Eighty men each. That's forty-eight hundred in all."

"A full legion."

Braden shook his head in wonderment. "A whole Roman Legion from the first century." Then he glanced at Morley. "Which legion?"

Morley's eyes twinkled in the glare of the floodlights. "Ah, that's yet another mystery. Follow me." He led Braden down the hallway toward the far end. Every door was open, and Braden glimpsed more bunks and people in white lab coats. Halfway down the hall, the ceiling and left-side wall had caved in, leaving a huge pile of broken stone on the floor. Yellow CAUTION tape had been erected around the debris. A sign proclaimed "Danger" and "Hardhats Must be Worn Beyond this Point" in three languages. He noticed a strong smell of decomposition, but it faded as they passed the area.

Morley stopped when he entered a huge chamber. "This is where we found most of the artifacts," he said, waving his hands toward long rows of tall racks and shelves. "Plate armor and helmets, weapons, marching gear, cooking implements, leather apparel. All in an excellent state of preservation."

Braden let his eyes wander around the big space. Banks of fluorescent lights illuminated long aluminum folding tables where more scientists and technicians were examining artifacts. He stopped to look at a stack of plate armor. "Lorica Segmentata," he murmured. "That's how you fixed the date at the first century?"

Morley nodded. "Yes. No chain mail was found. You probably know the Lorica Hemata was largely phased out by AD 50."

Braden ran his fingers over the cold metal bands. "This was state-of-the-art Roman armor. Very expensive."

"Only a few favored legions were able to obtain it. Senatorial influence helped." Then Morley pointed to a stack of weapons. "All those swords are as sharp as the day they were made. See for yourself. But be extremely careful."

Braden pulled a gladius from its scabbard. For a moment he recalled telling Ann about the scabbard, but when he saw the blade gleaming in the harsh lights, he felt a visceral twist in his stomach. What would it feel like to have one of these slicing into your belly? He shook his head and put the weapon back. "Were there any food rations?"

Morley pointed to a stack of terra-cotta jars and amphorae. "Not much. We found only traces of hard bread and meat. All the grain and dried fruit was gone. The wine had dried up ages ago."

At the nearest table, a woman was taking digital photographs of the interior of a bronze canister. It was about the size of a five-gallon drum. Then she carefully lifted out a tightly coiled belt. It was studded with rectangular bronze plates. "Apparently," Morley said, watching the woman, "all the leather gear was stored in canisters like that. Airtight, from what we can determine. Caligae, belts, cingulum, thongs, and even wool tunics were stored." He chuckled. "I could open a Roman Army surplus store with this lot."

Braden suddenly thought of these weapons turning up on eBay or the black market but refrained from mentioning it.

Morley led Braden to a table where a heavyset man was peering intently at the back of a shield. "Now, as to your question about which legion, I will show you what we have found." He tapped the man on the shoulder. "George, may I interrupt you for a moment?"

The man looked up and smiled. "Certainly, Arthur. What can I do for you?"

"This is Alex Braden, and I'd like to show him the face of the scutum. Can you turn it over for me?"

"Of course," George said, lifting the heavy shield. He carefully turned it over and rested it back on the table. "It has an unusual type of grip. I have to contact Holmes at Cranfield and find out if he has ever seen one like this." Then he picked up an iPad and began typing as Braden looked at the artifact.

The scutum was rectangular, over a meter tall, and deeply curved from side to side. It was a full centimeter in thickness. A heavy convex metal disk was set in the center like a 1950s hubcap. "What is the mystery?" Braden asked.

The older man pointed a finger at the center of the shield. "Look at the emblem."

Braden examined the red-painted face of the shield. Two pairs of golden wings, one above and one below, were interspersed with stylized lightning bolts. Across the center was a wide banner bearing the letters LEG.LIV VDCTA. "Legio . . . Fifty-four." He shot a look at Morley, who was watching him with an amused expression. "Fifty-four?"

Morley held out his hands. "I told you it's a mystery."

"But there never was a fifty-fourth legion," Braden protested.

"That's what we've all thought. No record of any legion past Legio Thirty Ulpia Victrix."

"Are all the others like this?"

"Yes," George interjected. "All thirty-six hundred."

Morley turned to his colleague. "You have a count?"

George held up his iPad. "Chester Hood, who has been doing an inventory just sent it to me. Thirty-six hundred and fifty scutum. And they all bear the same markings."

"How interesting," Morley said. He rubbed his chin. "Did he inventory anything else?"

George consulted the iPad again. "Yes, he has a count on swords and armor as well."

Morley peered at him over the glasses. "And?"

"Again, about thirty-six hundred of each."

The archaeologist sighed. "Another enigma. Bunks and quarters for forty-eight hundred legionaries but only enough weapons and armor for three-quarters that number."

Braden was watching the exchange. He felt a chill on his skin that had nothing to do with the cold air. There's more than a thousand missing. "Shit," he murmured under his breath. "Professor, was there ever an entire legion in here?"

Morley thanked George and led the way back out to the hall. "I'll tell you what we know, or at least what we think we know. As I said there are sixty rooms. So far, we found fourteen rooms whose bunks had been used as you saw in the first chamber."

Morley stopped at a door about a third of the way down the hall. "But another forty were like this."

Immediately, Braden realized something was different. He wrinkled his nose at the scent of decay and dust that hadn't been in the first room. The carved lettering on the lintel read Cohor. VIII, Cento. V. Inside were more bunks, but these didn't hold only moldering mattresses. On each one was a skeleton. The bones were a dusty brown color and lay as if on a medical school anatomy table. They were all clad in the tattered remains of wool tunics. The fabric had turned almost black. Every bunk held the same story. It was an army of skeletons. Braden moved closer. "Are these really the bones of Roman legionaries?"

"Yes, they are," Morley said. "One hundred and sixty of them. All in all, we've found forty rooms like this." Then he sighed. "But there's more, Alex. Much more."

"What do you mean?"

"Come and see." Morley turned and walked down the hall. The unpleasant odor Braden had noticed in the hallway grew stronger. It was the smell of decomposing flesh. He tried to breathe through his mouth. "God, what is that smell?"

"In here." Morley stopped at where the corridor wall had collapsed. The door was askew and splintered. The smell was coming from the room. The professor seemed not to notice it. "In here is the greatest mystery of all. Take a look."

Braden stepped closer while trying not to gag from the stench of putrefaction. Most of the room was buried under a huge slide of rock and dirt. The remaining ceiling inside was supported by heavy screw jacks and timbers. A large fan was running, but it failed to dissipate the odor. He saw three of Morley's team leaning over a set of bunks that had been crushed by fallen masonry. Then a man holding a digital camera moved aside to adjust the light and revealed a body. Braden gasped. The crushed remains of an adult male lay on the fragmented wooden bunk. Mottled gray flesh covered the torso and arms under fragments of blackish fabric. The dead man's face was almost intact. His hair was black and hung in long curtains over the heavily bearded face.

"My God . . ." Braden said in a whisper. He was looking at the crushed and decayed remains of a man who'd once been a citizen of Imperial Rome. The other bunks held more bodies. "It's not possible."

"We're finding rather a lot of impossible things in here," Morley said with a weak grin. "I'm quite coming to expect them."

"But the skeletons . . ." Braden began, then stopped.

"The skeletons in those other rooms have likely been dead for two thousand years. We'll know more after forensic examination. That should rule out what some of our people are calling a massive hoax."

Braden pointed at the Roman corpses. "But will it explain them?"

"We'll see. They are in an impossibly good state of preservation. It's as if they died only a few weeks ago." He pointed to the rockslide. "Six rooms are like this. And near the storeroom is a vacant room with about a dozen more bodies who might have been ill or diseased." He led Braden back to the hall. "The odor does get to me. Let's go back up for some fresh air."

They reached the base of the stairs, where more scientists were at work.

Braden's brow furrowed. What Morley had said triggered something in his mind, but just as he tried to concentrate on it, a man wearing a lab coat over a gray jumpsuit came up to Morley. He had a smooth, almost cherubic face. He carried a laptop computer. Braden pegged him as a computer geek.

"Arthur," the man said. "Can you spare a moment?"

"Of course, Benjamin. This is Alex Braden, an investigator from NATO. Alex, this is Doctor Benjamin Hawkins, one of our architectural archaeologists."

Hawkins gave Braden a polite nod. "I've got something interesting to show you."

"This is the day for it," Morley said. "Let's see what you have."

Hawkins opened the laptop. "I've been studying the ramp," he said, pointing to the massive incline of masonry. "I've been attempting to model the stones and figure out their construction. You recall we agreed it's strange the way they're laid alongside the stairs. If you look at the screen, you will see that it is made up of seventy-four very carefully shaped and interlocked blocks and wedges."

Braden looked at the screen and saw the 3-D image of the ramp. Each stone was a different color, so it looked as it was made of LEGO blocks.

Hawkins continued. "This puzzled me, if you'll forgive the pun, because it looks much like one of those Chinese wooden puzzles. I collect them, and I've never found one I couldn't beat."

Morley nodded. "I know, Benjamin. Go on."

Hawkins began, "Each block has two numerals carved in it. One number is the sequence for assembling the ramp. But they can also fit together in another way. I'll show you." He punched a key on the computer and an animation began. It showed the ramp disassembling itself in a complex dance into a long tapered square block.

"I see," said Morley, but it was clear he didn't.

Hawkins smiled. "The new configuration measures out as one meter square at one end and 2.15 meters at the other and is 4.83 meters in length. Do those numbers sound familiar?"

Braden realized Hawkins was enjoying stumping the team leader.

Morley's eyes narrowed. Then he brightened. "The entrance tunnel."

"Right," Hawkins said with a smile. "The second number on each block is the sequence for assembling the plug. It would fit the entry to the tunnel perfectly. The single large block at the top was the farthest into the tunnel."

"Evidently, it was never in place."

Hawkins shook his head. "Yes, it was. Until very recently. I asked our botanist, Beverly Perkins, to examine the stones. She found pollen and wild grains in between some of the blocks. They are more than a thousand years old. She is convinced the tunnel had been sealed."

Clearing his throat, Braden inquired, "Did someone open it from the outside?"

"Hold on, Mister Braden. Let me finish. Each piece would be placed in a certain spot on the floor with the others to assemble the ramp. When it was finished, the last large block could be pulled loose and slid onto it." Hawkins paused. "Therein lies the riddle, Arthur."

The professor cradled his chin in one hand. "I'm afraid I still don't understand."

Hawkins sighed. "I've modeled it a dozen times, and I'm convinced I'm right. But for the life of me, I can't imagine how it can be true."

Morley waited.

"The plug could only be removed from one end."

"And what way is that?" Morley asked, mystified.

"From the inside."

CHAPTER XIII

A STONE ENIGMA

Braden and Morley sat under the wide marquee. A cool breeze drifted in and rustled the papers on the tables. Morley sipped a glass of red wine. André Robert was happy to have such a prestigious expedition on his land and had donated several cases to the team. Braden opted for a Coke.

"So what do you have down there, Professor? What exactly is it?"

Morley regarded the deep red liquid in his glass. "In a nutshell, it's a Roman riddle, a . . ." He paused, thinking, "an Etruscan enigma, a masonry mystery." He grinned. "Ah, wine makes me so whimsical."

Braden said, "Hawkins said it could only have been opened from below. That means the people inside the cellar opened it. And that had to have been centuries ago."

"I'm afraid not," Sharon said as she entered the shade of the marquee. Both men looked up at her.

"Beverly Perkins examined the stones in the ramp and found pollen, grain, and other organic materials in cracks and fissures. She sent them to the lab in Paris for dating and identification." She sat down in a chair next to Morley and turned on her iPad. "I just received her results. The oldest samples range from more than sixteen hundred years, plus or minus three hundred years. One plant was a species of wild grass that's been extinct in the region since the tenth century."

Morley and Braden exchanged confused looks at this.

Sharon pulled a bottle of water from the cooler and took a long swig. She saw their expressions. "No way those grains got into the cracks and fissures in the rock down in the cellar. There's no doubt the ramp stones had been used to seal the entrance. That stone plug was in place for at least sixteen centuries, Arthur. Probably more like twenty. I'm sure of it."

"You're saying it may have been opened recently?" Braden asked. He thought of the missing weapons.

Sharon finished her water and expelled a repressed belch. "Yes, I believe so."

"But how recently?"

"We found lots of stripped grape bunches in the cellar. André Robert said they were chardonnay from the upper hillside. They were mature vines and picked less than two weeks ago."

"Someone was inside before Robert found it." Braden shook his head in frustration.

Morley put down the glass. "It would have taken a large team of men working with heavy block and tackle to move those stones. Robert would not have missed it."

"How long has he been on this land?" Braden asked.

Morley looked at the vineyard on the hill. "His great-grandfather first established the vineyard in 1905. Before that, it was a virgin forest that went back to the early Middle Ages." He poured himself some more wine. "Back to your question, what we have down there is a large extensive barracks and storage cellar. It held exactly forty-eight hundred men and all their marching equipment."

Braden mulled this over. "An army travels on its stomach. What about food?"

Sharon answered him. "Hundreds of bronze containers had been found in the big room which once contained dried meat, hardtack, and fruit. But it was little more than dust. A small amount was found in three of the empty rooms. Some of that seems to have survived the ages."

"Food that was edible after two thousand years?" Braden said.

"I wouldn't try it myself, but it was still safe to eat."

Braden sipped his Coke and grinned. "Amazing. How much was there altogether?"

"Hard to say exactly," Morley said. "Enough rations, I presume, to sustain a legion for a week of marching."

"That's not very much," Braden pointed out.

"No, it is not. But a Roman Legion could easily supplement their rations with foraging and hunting. So it's not too hard to justify." He paused. "Which brings me back to your original question and a great contradiction. What do we have down there?"

Braden gave him a slight shrug. "As you suggested, a cellar for sleeping."

"And nothing else," Morley said. "No bathing or toilet facilities, no kitchen. It was just for one purpose. For a legion to sleep and then march on. It was clearly not for an extended stay since I cannot imagine an entire legion living here for days or weeks without a bathroom. Can you?" He smiled and sipped his wine.

"Hardly," Braden grinned. Again, he felt he was missing something important but couldn't get a fix on it. "And the contradiction?"

"Yes," the older man said, looking pointedly at Braden. "There were almost five thousand bronze canisters with tightly sealed lids. Some are empty but most contained leather gear and clothing. All the metal objects were left on racks and shelves, but the leather gear was sealed. For what reason, I cannot say, but it would account for their remarkable state of preservation."

Braden waited.

Then Morley raised an eyebrow. "So, if there was no intention of a long stay, why have leather equipment stored in heavy containers that would preserve them?"

"That is strange," Braden agreed.

Morley shook his head. "I've been researching and excavating Roman sites for thirty years. This is the biggest and most complex mystery I've ever come across. A challenge like this I can do without at my age."

"Oh, Arthur," Sharon scoffed. "You thrive on challenges. So try this on for size. Why would the plug be so damned tight?"

"What do you mean, Sharon?"

"Ben told me that when it was in place, the seal would have been absolutely airtight, like an Egyptian tomb. The air inside was first-century air."

"Airtight?" Morley asked. "That doesn't make any sense. I can see them wanting some solid seal to keep the local Gauls out, but airtight?"

Braden thought this over. "Five degrees Celsius. Dry air. And totally sealed from the outside world." He cocked his head. "You mentioned an Egyptian tomb. Perhaps it was meant to be a tomb."

Morley shook his head. "Then why the mattresses? The food? The sealed leather equipment? It does not fit, Alex." Morley leaned back in his chair. "Bloody hell. Nothing fits. Every single element has something that negates it. An unknown legion in an underground barracks without bathrooms. Sealed in an airtight icebox with food and weapons. How did thirty-six hundred men die? Why are some only skeletons and others appear as if they died a week ago last Saturday?" He took another drink and expelled a breath. "And if they were dead, who the bloody hell opened the cellar from the inside?"

"The missing twelve hundred legionaries did," Braden commented.

For several moments Morley and Sharon stared at him. Then Sharon started to laugh. Morley joined her. After a minute he had to set down his glass and wipe his eyes. "Ah, I needed that. Thank you, Alex."

Braden grinned sheepishly. "Sorry, it just popped out. I was just thinking we've forgotten something."

"Just the one thing?" Morley asked with a half-smile.

"Fourteen rooms had been used but are empty," Braden began slowly. "Forty more hold only skeletons. And six were crushed but probably held 480 more."

"Right," Morley agreed.

"All you can account for is thirty-six hundred legionaries."

Morley gave him a nod.

Braden looked pointedly at him. "So what happened to the other twelve hundred?"

The two scientists looked at each other. "Ah, well," Morley said, "that's hard to say."

"I'm sure it is," Braden said. "But the fact remains that at least a thousand weapons and marching gear are missing, and so are twelve hundred men."

Sharon spoke up. "You're an investigator, Alex. What does your experience tell you?"

"That someone had gotten into the cellar before Robert found it and stole the weapons."

"And twelve hundred bodies?" Sharon asked.

"We can't rule it out. Grave robbing is as old as civilization itself."

"Okay," Sharon said, "but how did they get in when the stones could only be removed from the inside?"

Braden shrugged. "I can't figure that one either. But no case is ever airtight. There are always inconsistencies. History has shown us that nearly every solved case has at least one major element that doesn't fit and never will. No investigator is infallible."

"How about Sherlock Holmes?" asked Morley with a wry grin.

Braden sighed. "Not even him. Remember it took almost a century before anyone figured out who Jack the Ripper was."

"A female crime fiction author solved it," Sharon said.

"Yeah," Braden said. "Ironic, isn't it? Anyway, every case has some loose ends. Perhaps there is another way into the cellar."

Morley shook his head. "Won't wash, Alex. We've been over the entire site inside and out. There is no other tunnel."

"Damn." Braden wiped his face. "Legio Fifty-four. That's another unfathomable mystery."

"Yes," Morley agreed. "Out of everything we've found, that is the one that does not fit the historical record."

"Thirty Roman Legions," Braden said, looking at the black pit. "What happened to the other twenty-three?"

Morley shrugged. "If we can prove the artifacts are authentic, it will change the entire history of the Roman Army. If I wasn't so confident in our techniques for dating artifacts, I'd almost believe the cellar was the set for some long-forgotten movie."

Braden chuckled. "Yeah. I heard that some of George Lucas's sets from the Star Wars movies caused a sensation a few years ago when they were 'discovered' by some amateur archaeologists in the Tunisian desert."

"Ah, yes. That was amusing."

"You're sure of the dating?" Braden asked, draining his Coke.

Morley nodded emphatically. "Very. Our equipment is the best. We ran mass spectrometry and Carbon-14 on a random sampling of leather and cloth artifacts. The radio-carbon levels date them to between 2,005 and 2,020 years. Nothing under that range. The scutum are the newest at 2,005 years old."

"Okay," Braden said, "but what does 'VDCTA' mean?"

Morley sat up. "Ah, our Latin specialist is working on that right now. And she's come up with some words that might fit, but none of them make sense. It might be an honorific name, such as Legio Twenty Augustus."

"May I see the list?"

"Certainly," Morley said, turning in his chair to leaf through a pile of folders. "I don't like those iPad things. I like holding paper." He handed a folder to Braden. "Here you go." He poured himself another glass of wine. "Bloody good vintage. At least something good came from this bizarre muddle."

Braden scanned the list. There were a dozen words beginning with "V" and ending in "A," including vagina, which made him grin. Then he came to the last word in the list.

VINDICTA: Vengeance *ulciscor ulcisci ultus dep.*

1: to take vengeance for, avenge, to punish.

VINDICTA: deliverance; vengeance; punishment.

Deep in his stomach, Braden felt a chill.

Plutonius's scouts found an excellent place to hide for the day. It was a dense part of a forest that sloped down to the east toward the valley of the Rhenus River. Shortly after sunrise, a thick fog swept in from the river, obscuring everything around them. Even the tops of the pine trees disappeared in the white mist. A heavy gray overcast blotted out the cold sun, and Lucius smelled more rain in the damp air.

"This is the best place we have ever found to conceal ourselves," he said. He ordered Regulus and his invaluable archers to form a perimeter around the legion. "If you see anyone, loose an arrow into the camp, but do not call out. If we are fortunate, they may pass by and miss us."

The archers saluted and moved off. In seconds they were swallowed by the fog.

Lucius pointed to a patch of bare earth. "Now let us make use of this cover and cook our pork."

"In the daytime?" Septimus asked.

"Yes. I do not want a repeat of what happened after we came into Belgicae. With this fog we can dig fire pits and roast the pig meat. We will cover the pits with damp blankets until the meat is done, then douse the coals."

"I will see to it." Septimus walked away to find Vitellus.

Marcus spoke up. "We should reach the river by midnight."

"That is good," replied Lucius as he looked around the groups of legionaries. "Have you heard anything more from Sestus about Atticus?"

Marcus shook his head. "Not since we met the two men in the forest. He has been quiet. But I am sure he is thinking only dark thoughts."

Lucius gave an irritated shake of his head. "I do not care what is in his mind as long as it does not come from his mouth."

"Sestus is loyal to you and our cause. He will keep you informed."

"Sometimes I look at young Sestus and see myself. So eager, so impulsive."

The big man smiled. "Were you ever that way?"

Then it was Lucius's turn to smile. "Yes, I was very rash. I did foolish and dangerous acts that I am still amazed that I survived." He glanced at Marcus. "Can any of us claim otherwise?"

"Certainly not I, Lucius Cassius," the big man said with a knowing grin.

A short time later, the rich smell of wood smoke and roasting meat tickled Lucius's nose. "We shall eat like kings, my friend." He put the sword away and walked over to the nearest pit. A dozen legionaries were holding wet blankets over the large hole. Only a small amount of fragrant smoke emerged and mingled with the fog.

Vitellus pointed at the nearest pit. "This one is nearly done, Sire. I will pull it out and we can divide the meat."

"Pass the first cuts to the archers on sentry duty," Lucius said. "Each cohort may have a whole pig. We can carry the rest."

After the juicy pork had been divided among the three cohorts, the fires were doused. "This fog was a gift from the gods," said Marcus, using his pugio to cut meat from a thigh bone. "For the first time, I feel safe during the day."

"Get some rest as soon as you eat," Lucius said, finishing the last of his own meal. "We still have the river to cross."

The day passed quietly. No one intruded on the legion's rest. But Lucius was awake and thinking about what lay ahead. Germania. They were almost there.

The fog dissipated by mid-afternoon. The gray overcast made the sun into a pale glow that grew dimmer as it sank behind the trees to the west. Septimus walked over to Lucius. His face was grave. "Sire, we have lost six more men."

Lucius sighed. "Very well, Septimus Deo. Have them buried in the pits. It is not dignified, but it is the best we can do."

Septimus nodded. "All six men were from Cohort Apollo."

"Ah. I see. That means Atticus will again begin his vitriolic diatribes about our cause."

"He is already doing so. Sestus took me aside while I was talking to the medicus. Atticus is angry at losing more men. For some reason his cohort has a higher percentage of dying men than either Mars or Jupiter."

Lucius admitted that was curious. "I wonder why that would be so? Are they receiving the same rations as the other men?"

"They are," Septimus said. "I cannot find any logical reason for it. The only commonality is that most of Apollo's legionaries came from Cohorts Tertius and Quintus."

Lucius mulled this over. "That may explain it. Quintus lost more than three-quarters their number because of Julius Plinus not heeding Gothicus Romulus's advice."

"If that is so, there is nothing we can do for them."

"No, nothing," Lucius said. "If they were to find out they have a greater chance of dying on the march than the others, they may revolt."

Marcus arrived in time to hear the exchange. "I will tell Sestus to watch the men carefully. He is from Cohort Secundus, so he may not be at risk."

"Very well," said Lucius. He looked at the darkening sky. "We will resume the march in an hour."

CHAPTER XIV

ALCHEMISTS

"This place is just right for doffing the stress of the work," Morley said to Braden and Sharon as they seated themselves in a small country restaurant a few kilometers from Robert's vineyard. After a long day of discoveries and frustration, the elderly archaeologist had decided on the spot to invite them out for an evening dinner. Braden had not eaten anything since leaving Brussels and readily agreed.

"It is nice," Sharon agreed. She was wearing a blue pants suit with her long hair draped over her shoulders. Morley was dressed in a tweed jacket and white shirt with bow tie that suited him perfectly. Braden was still in the gray slacks and black polo shirt he'd worn all day.

A waiter came and they ordered drinks, none of which turned out to be wine. Braden's Screwdriver, Sharon's Fuzzy Navel, and Morley's gin and tonic arrived a few minutes later. They ordered their entrees and talked about traveling and history.

"So," Morley said as he cut his fish, "what did you think of our little dig?" He ate with characteristically British neatness and daintiness.

"It was extremely fascinating," Braden said. "I learned a great deal and very much enjoyed the experience." He finished his soup, and the waiter whisked away the bowl with an efficient sweep. "I have a lot to think about."

"Ah, don't we all," Morley agreed.

"I'm afraid you found more than you bargained for," said Sharon, who was picking at her salad as if she weren't really interested in the food.

Braden nodded. "Yes, that's true. But I'm more convinced than ever that some weapons were taken from the cellar."

Morley frowned. "And used to kill two police officers?"

"Possibly," Braden said. "To be honest, the source of the weapons is less important at this time than the identity of the murderers. The break-in of the cellar is not in my jurisdiction unless I can prove a link."

"Yes," Morley said. "That would come under the French National Police."

Braden sipped his drink and tapped a finger on the tablecloth. "My next job is to find them. And if they are carrying Roman weapons, then we can learn their source. But I don't know how long that will take. In the meantime, we have no way to determine where the weapons came from."

Sharon cut in. "I have an idea." She looked at Braden seriously. "I was reading the report you gave us from the coroner on those dead policemen. It piqued my curiosity. I took some measurements of the weapons we had gathered for studies. A random sample since all the swords are apparently the same type. And the pila as well."

"And?" Morley watched her attentively.

"From the measurements I gathered, the stab and penetration wounds are exactly the right size."

The older man wiped his lip with his napkin before he spoke. "That's hardly surprising. The weapons are nearly identical in size and shape. The reenactment groups use reproduction Roman swords, and they could fit perfectly as well."

"I realize that, Arthur, but we know for a fact these are Type VI Gladius España, also known as the Harris-Germanicus Sword. They were comparatively rare in the Roman Army. Only six have ever been found. They represent a fraction of the weapons known to exist. The Type VI is a virtually unknown version of the sword, and not many people, even historians, know it exists. This makes identifying the murder weapons easier."

Braden was listening carefully. She seemed to be leading up to something important.

"I'm listening," Morley smiled. He wasn't in the least perturbed to have his own opinion challenged. He showed respect for his colleague's views.

Sharon continued. "The chances of our weapons matching the exact dimensions of those being used by someone unconnected with the cellar is almost impossible."

"Why is that?" Braden asked.

"There are sixteen known types of Roman short swords, from early Republic to the late fourth-century period. The most common is the older pattern, nowadays known as Mainz-Fulhams, which were clearly derived from the old gladius Hispaiñensis. They had a gradually tapering blade with a long point suited for ripping open chain mail." Sharon paused. "The first known one was discovered in northern England in 1821. This type represents by far the most widely used of the weapons in the Roman Army. The newer pattern, with the modern designation of Pompeii type, had a straight edge with a shorter point. This design was connected to the fact that the Roman Army was more often faced by unarmored barbarians rather than the mailed troops fielded by organized armies. Twenty-three of them have been found and identified since then. Only six of the remaining fourteen Roman swords have been Type VI Harris-Germanicus." She gathered steam. "The odds of a weapon as rare as they come and sharp enough to have killed so efficiently, and at this specific time being unconnected with this discovery, are virtually zero. Alex is right. The weapon or weapons used in the killings came from the cellar."

Morley considered this as he rubbed his eyes. "That is disturbing. I don't like what it implies. If artifacts have been removed from the cellar, this taints the entire find. It means we cannot trust anything we find or examine." He ran his fingers through his gray hair. "Blast! If there weren't already enough headaches from this bloody mess. Now we have to be even more careful. Who knows what the bastards took or what they might have left behind. Nothing can be trusted."

"I don't believe we have to go that far, Arthur," Sharon said in a reassuring voice. "The find is relatively untainted, but some artifacts are gone. We may never know how many or what. But once we've examined everything, we can prove the rest of the find is valid."

Morley shook his head. "It won't be that easy. This is a truly monumental find. Every detail will be gone over with a fine-tooth comb. And woe betide us if we can't validate every single artifact or conclusion. If you are correct, some of these things may soon show up on the artifact black market. Even on eBay."

Braden suddenly felt guilty for adding to Morley's frustrations. He hadn't told them about the strange sightings of "Romans" moving through France and Belgium. So far, he'd only said that Roman-type weapons had been used. What would Morley say if he knew that men wearing Roman armor were marching east in the night? That their origin might have been the very cellar he was studying? He looked at Sharon. "Is there any way to confirm or deny the origin of the weapons used in the murders?"

"I think so," Sharon said. "Microscopic traces of metal might be found on the bones of the policemen. The coroner can do a spectrographic analysis. If the metallic content matches that of our weapons, then we have a valid connection. If it is different, the murder weapons are probably modern reproductions. There would be a tangible difference."

Morley looked at Braden, a ray of hope showing on his face. "Is that possible?"

"I can call Doctor Montrose and ask. The backbone of one of the officers had been broken by the pilum which struck him and might have metal slivers or smears on it. It's definitely worth a try." He glanced at Sharon, grateful for her support. "If the weapons are reproductions, then the cellar is clean, Professor." He hoped this would be the case since it wouldn't make any difference in his investigation whether the sword and spear were authentic Roman weapons or reproductions. It would at least eliminate one source.

"I hope so too, Alex. I think we can arrange to have a sample of the weapons sent to the coroner."

"Great." Braden picked up his drink. The ice had long since melted. "I hope this discovery will go unchallenged and be the crown jewel of your work, sir."

The other man accepted the toast with a modest nod of his head. Then he turned back to Sharon with a smile. "Are there any other bombshells you wish to drop, my dear?"

Sharon shrugged. "Just one, but it could wait until tomorrow. I'm sure Alex wouldn't be interested."

"Please, go right ahead," Braden said. "This is still fascinating." He signaled the waiter for another round of drinks. Morley opted for a brandy.

"Well, it has to do with my study of the bronze bowls in the barracks rooms," she began. "I've been trying to find some explanation for them."

"Yes, that has been puzzling as well," the professor said. "Go on."

"There are three thousand altogether. Each of the sixty barracks rooms has fifty bowls arranged around all four walls. They are large enough to hold six liters of fluid, but they only have that burned matter in them."

"Are they some kind of lamp?" Braden asked.

"I'm not sure," Sharon admitted. "I'll tell you what Beverly Perkins told me. She specializes in botany. They contained a burnt residue of a water plant called Liliacae Mallorcus, native to southern France and the marshes along the Adriatic Sea. It's rare now, but in Roman times, it was far more abundant. It has some very interesting clinical properties."

"Such as?" Morley inquired.

"Beverly said it's being studied by medical researchers. It's a powerful sleep narcotic and being considered for possible use as a cryogenic hibernation agent. Anyone who ingests it will become comatose for a long period. It greatly slows the metabolism and brain wave activity, close to death. It also has some remarkable effects on aging by retarding the formation of free radical damage and arteriosclerosis, among other things."

"Interesting," Morley said. "Please continue."

"Beverly found some references in ancient texts that mention the plant as being used for a food preservative. A cut of meat soaked in the brine of Mallorcus will last for years. In fact, that may be why some of the food survived."

"That's the stuff burned in the bowls?" Braden asked.

"Yes. It was in the form of a highly concentrated paste, almost like wet plaster. Beverly estimated about eighteen hundred liters of the plant mixture were burned. Liliacae Mallorcus has enough oils in it to burn with a very strong white smoke, like incense. A gram of it would burn for about six hours or so."

"How much was in each bowl?" Morley asked.

"About five to six liters in each. Bev estimated it would have burned for at least five months."

"Remarkable," Morley said, sipping his brandy.

Sharon continued. "Smoke is essentially the light carbon residue of a burned material. Hydrocarbon or oil smoke is heavy and falls to earth in time. But the Mallorcus smoke has a low specific gravity, almost as light as oxygen. It would be suspended almost indefinitely, drifting in the air and moving only from the Brownian Motion of molecules and temperature inversions."

Braden thought about the sealed cellar and closed rooms. Every room contained bunks. That smoke would have permeated the cold air and hung there for months. "Maybe those legionaries used the plant that way. Maybe they put themselves to sleep." It had just been a thought, but he couldn't leave it unsaid.

"Unlikely," Sharon said, shaking her head. "They might only have used it for some ritual purpose, a sort of cleansing of the cellars. There are probably other properties of the plant unknown to modern science." She picked up her fork, again turning her attention to the now-limp salad. "The Romans were very clever, Alex. They've forgotten more than we'll ever learn about herbology and alchemy."

Braden's investigator mind was urging him to learn more. "I understand that, Sharon. But try this on for size. Just suppose someone were to be in a closed environment with this smoke. What would happen?"

Sharon smiled. "It'd put them out right quick," she said. "And they'd sleep like the dead. Literally. Until the residue was purged from their systems."

"How long would it take?"

Sharon chewed thoughtfully for a moment. "I suppose it depends on how much they inhaled, the relative humidity, air temperature, and a lot of other variables. The heart rate would go down to perhaps two or three beats per hour, and respiration would be less than one an hour. The body's metabolism and brain activity would come to a virtual stop. So it might take a few years or even decades. But of course they'd die sooner or later without some way of monitoring their vital signs."

"What about the carbon dioxide build-up?" Braden asked. "Seems it would reach toxic levels at some point."

She nodded. "Interestingly, the plant acts in the manner of lithium hydroxide and absorbs the CO_2 from the air. I don't know the details, but as long as the carbon dioxide is scrubbed from the air, the oxygen would be breathable."

"They could live for many decades," Morley commented.

"Decades?" That was a long time. But not as long as two millennia. Braden's forehead creased. Why had he thought that? He felt a tickle at the back of his neck, that tiny indicator that he was missing something important. "Okay, but is it possible to survive that long without food or water? Wouldn't the brain die from lack of oxygen?"

"Not necessarily," Sharon said, running a finger through the condensation on her glass. "The brain waves would be almost flat. All activity and need for oxygen would be curtailed to a high degree. The person would simply be in a coma."

Braden persisted. "And if the smoke were not purged? I mean, what if the smoke remained in a closed system?"

"They'd never wake up. They'd be in a coma until their bodies simply wasted away."

"And that could take decades?"

She shrugged. "I guess. Perhaps several."

"What are you driving at, Alex?" Morley inquired.

"Nothing specific," he admitted. "This is so weird. It's just that these bowls filled with a potentially lethal plant were placed by the thousands in a cellar that housed a legion of troops in a manner that would carry the smoke to every single nook and cranny. The cellar had an airtight plug and held nothing but bunks. You found skeletons in some rooms and bodies in others. And some rooms were empty. It's strange." He still felt like he was missing a critical piece of information.

"It is rather perplexing," Morley admitted, sipping the last of his brandy. "Yet in time we'll come up with a reasonable explanation."

"I hope you're right, Professor," Braden said without conviction.

CHAPTER XV

THE RHINE FRONTIER

Lucius looked at the water before him. He was standing on a shallow bluff, its slopes running down to the river's edge. The color of the wide estuary was impossible to determine in the darkness, but to Lucius, it would always be red. Red with the blood of Romans who crossed it in bitter defeat. He stared at the wide river before him. The black waters were surging with the current. Several boats and large craft were visible, some moving downstream while others churned their way south against the current.

He looked to the north. Ten miles downriver the lights of cities glowed like distant white forest fires along the banks. Some lights moved while others were long strings that followed the riverbank. He was amazed at the difference from ages past. "I see bridges and many, many big structures," he said, pointing.

The perils of the new world were a constant threat to them. Shortly after beginning their march to the river, they had come upon a wide road. It was brightly lit with orange lamps on tall poles. Dozens of large and small vehicles sped past with their brace of white and red lamps. After studying the vehicles for a time from the cover of thick brush, Septimus determined that there was a pattern to the flow. There were long pauses when there were no vehicles coming from one direction or another. Seizing the opportunity, Lucius had his men organize into groups of fifty men each. They were ready to dash across the road when Septimus gave the signal. The far side of the road dropped steeply toward the river.

Beyond the road was another of the strange sets of metal rails spiked to concrete ties. Almost half the legion had crossed when they heard a strident howling wail that cut through the night like a thousand daemons. It grew louder as a rhythmic clattering sound was accompanied by a deep thrumming noise coming closer. Every man froze where he stood, weapons at the ready. Then a searing white light tore through the darkness. Lucius gawked at the huge metal machine that roared toward them on the rails. It was huge and moved with frightening speed. As it blasted past them in a blizzard of noise and roiled air, Lucius forced himself to watch. It was followed by ten, twenty, fifty, a hundred large metal carriages on wheels. At last, the huge procession passed, leaving only the diminishing sound of clattering.

It had taken nearly two hours, but when the last legionary of Cohort Apollo scrambled down the embankment, all that lay before them was the west bank of the Rhenus River.

Marcus squinted into the blackness. "The riverbank is empty of lights for ten miles in either direction. If we are to cross, it must be here."

Lucius said nothing. From the southeast came the rumble of thunder. Dark clouds moved in, and in minutes, the storm was pelting the black surface. This was a relief and a curse to the tired legionaries. They might not be seen, but they still had no way to cross the wide river.

Lucius saw a brightly illuminated vessel moving downstream on the far side. He continued to watch until it disappeared into the rain-swept night.

Septimus looked to Lucius. "How may we cross? This will not be nearly as easy as the last three rivers we forded. They were mere rivulets against this."

"We will cross," Lucius said, speaking at last. He turned to his friend. "Do you remember the barges the army used to bring supplies to the forts? They could carry an entire centuria with little effort."

"Yes, I remember," Septimus admitted. "But with no fort to supply, we have no barge to use."

"Not to worry," said Marcus. "I think I see what our leader has in mind." He pointed upriver to a spot on the bank almost hidden by the crest of the bluff.

Septimus peered into the dark gloom. He saw a large black shape huddled close to the riverbank. Two lights, one red and one green, were reflected in the rippling black water. "What is it?"

Rain was pattering loudly on their helmets and armor, making conversation difficult, but he heard Lucius's words.

"It is our transportation," Lucius said, smiling at last.

A few minutes later, they were heading down a trail toward the river. By the time they reached the bank, the rain had turned the water's surface into a boiling cauldron. A few meters out on the water rested a huge black shape. It looked as big as a wine storehouse.

"A barge," Septimus said in awe. "So huge."

"Is it truly capable of sailing on the water?" Sestus asked.

"I think so," said Lucius. "See how it rises and falls with the current. It is far larger than any barge I remember, and it will carry us all."

"How will we move it?" Marcus asked. "It has no sails or oars. There is no tow-path on this bank. And we have no mules."

Lucius pointed past the immense barge. "There is another craft tied to it. See the lights? There are men on it. They will move it." He grinned. "After we convince them to do so."

Captain Heinrich Stauffen sat on a chair in the warm, dry cabin he shared with his first mate, Franz Kleist, on the river towboat *Rhein König-in*. He was a spare man of fifty-one, dark-haired with weathered skin. A former mate on a Deutsches Kriegsmarine salvage tug, Stauffen had earned his master's credentials twenty years before. He'd chosen towboats over other more exciting careers for one reason: He loved the Rhine. It was his river, having grown up on its banks in Bonn, watching it every day on his way to school. He knew its every twist, shoal, and mood. The cool lazy waters ran through his veins like no other body of water he'd ever known. As a boy, he'd read most of Mark Twain's works and fully understood the love a man could have for a river. The Rhine was no less worthy than the Mississippi. Yes, it was boring at times, but once in a while, during a gale, when some damn fool skipper of a tour boat decided to push his luck on the tricky currents and ended up in front of Stauffen's boat, it could get exciting.

But those times were rare. He held a large steaming mug of meat and vegetable soup made by Bendini, the Italian steward. The crew hardly understood his speech, but his cooking made any difficulties worthwhile.

"Ah," Stauffen said, sipping the thick, rich broth. "As far as I'm concerned, this storm can last all night. We're not due in Rotterdam until 1400 the day after tomorrow. We can afford to lose a night." Outside, a high-pressure system off the Dutch coast was unleashing 20-knot winds and rain down the Rhine Valley.

Rhein Königin was anchored on the west bank, twenty kilometers north of Koblenz. She was thirty meters in length with a ten-meter beam and had more than enough muscle in her four 5,000-horsepower diesels to push even the most heavily laden barges down the river to the Dutch coast. The large variable-pitch propellers could churn the placid blue waters of the Rhine into kilometers of muddy foam.

"I am almost glad that wind gust damaged the radar. It gave me an excuse to anchor here for the night."

The storm was expected to last for another thirty-six hours. Stauffen was used to navigating in rough weather but not without radar.

"Do you hear me complaining, Heinrich?" the first mate said over his own hot soup.

Stauffen chuckled. Kleist was only twenty-three, but a good man at the helm. He just needed some seasoning. *He'll be ready for my job in a few years if he learns to keep his temper under control.* The owner of a Rotterdam bar had almost pressed charges three months ago when the mate had a disagreement with a Belgian container ship officer, nearly wrecking the place. Time and a good teacher would do the job. Hard fists certainly hadn't.

"What did the home office say when you told them?" Kleist asked.

Stauffen smiled. "They weren't happy. But I am in command. Pushing a thousand-ton barge loaded with two thousand tons of lumber downriver without radar isn't worth the risk." He inhaled the aroma of the soup, then closed his eyes and listened to the rain beating on the cabin roof. "Is the watch on deck?"

Kleist peered out the front window. "It's not easy to see, but I don't think so. They're probably having soup in the wardroom."

Stauffen felt the towboat rock in the current. "The river will rise later. I want August and Klaus to check the anchors every hour."

Kleist picked up the phone and jabbed a button. "Klaus? Franz. The captain wants you and August to check the anchors every hour. Yes, thank you." He saw Stauffen holding up his empty mug. "Oh, and have Bendini bring us some more soup." He hung up.

"Thanks," said Stauffen.

"I wanted some too. He said they would do it shortly. By the way, does your wife know we're waiting out the night?"

"I called Katrina after notifying the home office." The sound of the rain grew louder. "It will be noisy tonight."

"And boring," came the reply from the younger man.

Stauffen sat down on his bunk and leaned back. "I have no problem with that."

Lucius, Marcus, Septimus, Plutonius, Crassius, and Sestus huddled in the thick brush at the river's edge with half a dozen legionaries. They were a stone's throw from the huge barge. It towered over their heads, a virtual wall of black steel. The cargo was covered in heavy tarps. The smaller boat Lucius had seen was nestled against the steel craft like a baby huddled for warmth on the belly of its mother.

"I do not see anyone on the deck," Marcus said. He wiped the rainwater from his face.

"In this weather? I think not," Septimus grunted, keeping his head lowered to avoid the worst of the wind-driven rain. "This craft has neither sails nor oars."

"The men on board will know how to move it," Lucius said. "Marcus, take three men and look into the windows. If you think you can take control of the boat, then do so. But be quiet, I urge you."

The big man scoffed. "No one could hear us if we were singing." But he took off his armor and handed it to a legionary. He motioned for Plutonius, Crassius, and Sestus to do the same. The Romans waded into the water, with Marcus leading the way. The churning water was up to his waist when he reached the ladder on the side of the craft. He pulled himself up the steel rungs and stepped carefully onto the wooden deck. The rest followed him. Rainwater ran off the deck and cabin roof in streams. Marcus drew his gladius and peered into a round porthole. The room beyond was as wide as the boat and contained chairs and upholstered benches. Three men sat around a table playing some sort of game with square cards displaying black and red symbols. One man laughed and swept up a small pile of papers. Then a fourth man entered the room carrying a tray of bowls. He put four bowls on the table then walked through a door toward the front of the boat. A minute later he reappeared and sat down with the others.

Marcus motioned for his men to approach. "Four men seated inside. There is another door on the far side of the room. Plutonius and Crassius, go to the other side. Sestus and I will stay here. Watch for me. When I go in, you do the same on that side. We will have to take them fast. Do not kill any of them."

Both men nodded silently and moved off toward the rear of the boat. A few minutes later, Marcus saw a finger at the edge of the far porthole. The canny Plutonius was ready.

He carefully examined the doorknob, seeing it was a brass bar that appeared to revolve. "Follow me in," he said to Sestus. "Keep your gladius ready." He took a breath, twisted the handle, and shoved the door open.

The men at the table looked up when the two doors burst open and displayed exactly the same double-take.

"What in the hell . . . ?" August Wohlmeyer said, eyes wide in disbelief. The words died in his throat. Standing in the warm, dry wardroom were four men who looked as if they had come from a wet Hell. They wore sodden red tunics and sandals. Long, unkempt hair and scraggly beards gave them the appearance of wild demons. In their hands were long swords.

"Who are you?" Wohlmeyer asked, finding his voice again. "What do you want?"

Marcus quickly put the point of his sword to the startled man's throat. "If you move, I will kill you," he said in a menacing voice.

Wohlmeyer froze, again stunned into silence. His eyes snapped back and forth between his companions and the intruders.

The Italian cook said, "He say he kill you if you move."

"What?" Wohlmeyer croaked, not taking his eyes off the gleaming blade.

"He say, 'No move. Stay,'" the cook repeated. "He speak Latin. I study in school."

"Who are they?" the sailor croaked.

Bendini, though frightened, was proud to be the only one who could speak the intruder's language. "Who are you?" he asked in Latin to the big man.

Marcus turned in surprise but recovered quickly. "How many are on this craft?"

The question received an automatic response. "Six," he said. Bendini's Latin was better than his German.

"What did he say?" asked Wohlmeyer.

"He want know how many are on board boat. I tell him six."

"They must be terrorists," Klaus Steinmann hissed, keeping a wary eye on Plutonius, who was holding his gladius pointed at him. "We cannot let them take the boat."

"What do you expect us to do, Klaus?" Wohlmeyer asked.

Marcus looked at Bendini. "Who is the commander of the boat?"

Bendini said nothing but his eyes betrayed him. He glanced at a door in the forward bulkhead. Marcus nodded to Plutonius and Crassius, who turned and moved to the door. Then Steinmann spun and tried to grab Plutonius's wrist, but the deck was slippery from the water dripping off the intruders' clothing, and he lost his footing. He stumbled wildly and fell toward Plutonius, who reacted instinctively and sidestepped while jabbing the long point of his weapon under the sailor's ribs. A rasping moan escaped Steinmann's lips, and he grabbed at his killer's arms. He slid to the deck. A stream of blood ran from his body and pooled on the deck, slowly mixing with the rainwater.

Marcus reacted immediately. "Find the other two men and bring them here!" He grabbed Wohlmeyer by the collar. "Do not do anything. Do not move. You will not be harmed if you obey." He shot a look at Bendini, who translated in a shaky voice, seeing the pool of blood spreading from the body.

Plutonius and Crassius went to the door and opened it to find a short corridor leading to the darkened wheelhouse, where the rain-streaked windows distorted the running lights like broken mirrors. On the left was another door with light streaming out from the sill. Plutonius approached it and listened. He heard two voices. Nodding to Crassius he twisted the knob and smashed the door to one side.

Stauffen and Kleist jumped to their feet at the sudden intrusion. They wore identical expressions of shock. "What in the hell is this?" roared Kleist. "Who are you?"

Crassius shoved Kleist back against the desk and put the blade of his gladius against his throat. Kleist was immediately quiet.

Plutonius pointed his bloody gladius at Stauffen. "Come," he said. Stauffen gaped at the wet and macabre apparition before him. He realized their boring night had ended.

Lucius wondered what was taking so long. Had something gone wrong? He was about to send Septimus to find out when a figure came down the ladder and waded through the water to him. It was Crassius.

"Sire, we have taken the boat. All the crew are our prisoners."

Lucius was too good an officer to ask questions. "Very well. Septimus Deo, stay with the men until I send for you." When he entered the small wardroom, he saw three things right away. A dead man on the deck, five men wearing varied expressions of fear and anger on their faces, and Marcus holding one man by the arm.

"Which of these men is in command?" Lucius asked Marcus.

"Here," said Marcus. "The others are crew."

Lucius nodded and folded his hands behind his back. "I am Lucius Cassius Aquilius. What is your name?"

Stauffen guessed what the question was. "Captain Heinrich Stauffen. I'm in command of this craft. And you have killed one of my men."

Lucius looked to Marcus for an explanation. But another man replied. "I am the cook, sir," the Italian said meekly. "I know your words. He is the captain, and you kill his man."

Lucius regarded the man for a moment and turned to Marcus. He spoke with a note of anger. "How did this happen?"

Marcus explained and Lucius nodded curtly. "I see. It could not be helped." He turned to the Italian cook. "Tell the captain I am sorry for this man's death. He attacked my legionary, who defended himself. If you cooperate, this will not happen again."

The cook turned to Stauffen, whom he liked. "Captain, he is sorry Klaus is dead. Do not try to fight or more will die." It was not an accurate translation, but it was the best he could do.

Stauffen took a breath and nodded his assent.

Then his first mate leaned close. "Heinrich!" Kleist hissed. "They are threatening us!"

Stauffen knew his friend had never responded well to threats. "Don't do anything to provoke them, Franz." He looked at the man who'd spoken to him. "What do you want from us?"

"We have need of your boat. We need to go there, now." Lucius pointed out the starboard window.

"Where?" Stauffen said after hearing the translation. "To the coast?"

"No. Across the river."

Stauffen's eyes widened in stupefied surprise. "You want to cross the river? Why in the hell do you need us? All you have to do is go about twenty kilometers downriver and cross the damn bridge. You killed one of my men for this?" He was speaking too fast for the cook to translate, but he didn't care.

Lucius heard the angry words and the translation. "I have no time to waste. A bridge is out of the question."

"But the storm knocked out my radar," Stauffen protested. "The river is too busy for me to risk travel. I could run someone down. I'm not willing to risk that." He waited for the words to make their way to the strange man in red wool and metal armor.

"This I do not comprehend, Captain. We must go and I will accept no excuses."

Stauffen considered this, glancing at Kleist's glowering face. "I can post lookouts, but it will be hard with the barge. We'll have to leave it behind and recover it later."

"The barge is the large square craft?"

"Yes."

"We have need of it. You cannot leave it."

"Why?" Stauffen asked.

"Because we are many, Captain. Many more than this," Lucius said, gesturing to the others.

"How many?"

Lucius told him.

Stauffen turned to Bendini. "Are you sure that's what he said? Eight hundred men?"

"Yes, Captain," Bendini said. "He say that."

"Who in God's name are you," the towboat captain demanded. "What you are doing is an act of piracy and murder. Punishable by life in prison. Why are you doing this?"

The cook struggled to translate, but Lucius stopped him. "Tell the captain I must do this. I have no choice. We have waited too long, have lost too many, and have too much to do to allow anything to stop us now. If he does not assist us, he must die, along with all of you." He said it coldly.

The cook, frightened by the words, translated them clearly.

Stauffen faced Lucius. "I don't understand, but I will do as you say if you promise none of my crew will come to harm."

Lucius said, "I will promise if no one attempts to fight or stop us. We are soldiers, not barbarians." He pronounced the last word with great rancor.

Stauffen's mind raced. He didn't know who these men were, what they wanted, or why they were dressed like this, but he believed they were deadly serious. He decided to cooperate and ask questions later. If there was a later. "I understand. I must issue orders to my crew." He turned to Kleist, who had murder in his eyes. Stauffen hoped the young firebrand would see how dangerous the situation was and remain cool. "Franz, do what I say, and we'll get through this alive. Warm up the diesels."

The first mate shot a look of pure hatred at Lucius and turned to walk into the wheelhouse. Plutonius was right behind him. Kleist checked the digital gauges and flipped several switches. He kept glancing at the blood-streaked weapon in Plutonius's hand.

Lucius turned to Marcus. "Marcus, tell Septimus to assemble the legion and board the barge. Tell them to move under those large tents," he pointed at the tarps covering the cargo. "They may find some shelter from the rain."

"As you order," Marcus said, leaving the room.

Stauffen looked at his two surviving deck crew. "Hans, August, I know you're angry about Klaus's murder, but if we cooperate, we'll live to see the dawn. After you check the towlines, you'll need to stand as lookouts. I'll tell you when to raise the barge's anchors. Watch for any craft. Their lights should be visible even in this rain. Put on your foul-weather gear, and take the radios with you." Then he had a thought. Maybe one of the lookouts could radio for help.

"I will have some of my legionaries watch your men," said Lucius as if he were reading Stauffen's thoughts.

They entered the wheelhouse, which was about five meters wide with big windows on three sides. The control panel and wheel dominated the center, with chart table, radios, and navigation equipment to either side. "Fuel lines are pressurized and warmed up, Captain," said Kleist. He held the wheel in a white-knuckled grip.

"Go ahead, Franz. Start her up." He kept his voice calm, trying to keep Kleist from becoming dangerously impulsive.

Kleist punched the four starter buttons. A series of strong vibrations ran through the hull. Lucius and the two legionaries started at the sudden vibration.

Stauffen peered past the windshield wipers at the barge, barely visible in the deck lights. His eyes went wide as hundreds of men carrying swords, spears, and shields climbed up the barge's ladders and burrowed under the heavy tarps. "My God," he gasped. "He wasn't joking." Where had they all come from? Who were they?

Half an hour later, Marcus came back in and nodded to Lucius, who in turn spoke to Stauffen. Bendini translated. "He say we go now."

"Very well," Stauffen said as he picked up the handset and told Hans and August to raise the barge anchors. A few minutes later, the huge craft wallowed in the current. "Push off, Franz," he said. The first mate engaged the propellers.

"Five hundred revolutions on the port engines, hard right rudder."

"Five hundred aye," said Kleist, as he worked the throttle levers and controls for the four stern rudders.

Stauffen leaned out the portside door and squinted at the churning water below. The *Rhein Königin*'s powerful diesels thrummed as she drove her bow against the thick rubber fenders that hung from the bluff barge's hull. A mass of white foam surged under her stern as she nudged the huge craft into the wide river. "Two meters under the keel," Kleist said. "We're clear of the bank."

Stauffen tried to see out the thick window, but even with the windshield wipers snapping back and forth, the rain turned the night into a mosaic of distant lights and shimmering haze. "Six knots and steady on, Franz," he said. "Make for the northbound lane. Not much traffic tonight." *Too bad a police boat couldn't show up now*, he thought. But they're more interested in terrorists and drug smugglers, neither of whom used large lumber barges. If he piloted recklessly, he might attract someone, but the risk to other boats was far greater than the off chance of a patrol coming along at the right moment.

Then two of the intruders carried Klaus's body out of the wardroom and dumped him overboard. Stauffen shot a look of fury at Lucius but remained silent. Klaus's body might be found and someone notice the manner of death. He carried identification. The limp corpse twisted and turned in the towboat's turbulent wake, then disappeared in the blackness.

"Where you wish to go, sir?" Bendini asked Lucius after being prompted by Stauffen.

"We need a place on the east bank that is quiet and uninhabited."

"That will be difficult," Stauffen replied. "There are many homes and docks on the east bank. Roads and rail lines run the entire length." But he knew of a few places that might suffice, and he wanted to get this group of madmen off his boat. "I know of a place about twelve kilometers downriver which might work. It was a sand and gravel company that went bankrupt a few years ago. It has been tied up in the courts and abandoned."

Kleist nodded, still watching out the dark windows. "I know the place. The dock was torn down, but the water is deep there."

"That's the place," Stauffen said. "We can get the barge right up to the bank." He described the place to Bendini, who translated.

Lucius nodded. "Take us there now, Captain."

Marcus and Sestus stepped into the wheelhouse and spoke to Lucius. Bendini leaned close to Stauffen and translated in a low voice. "He say some men are vomiting."

Lucius nodded and remained watching the black night beyond the windows.

Pushing its human cargo downstream, the towboat cut across the two-kilometer-wide river. The heavy downpour had not yet brought the high water and raging currents for which the Rhine was famous. The console radio crackled. "Small craft southbound on the starboard bow two hundred meters," said one of the lookouts. Stauffen picked up the handset, noting the way Lucius and the other men looked around for the source of the voice. "Very well." He pointed out the windows. "Steer five degrees port."

"Five degrees port aye." Kleist was cutting his eyes between the stormy night beyond the windows and the shelf under the control console. Stauffen saw this. There was a holstered 9mm Beretta pistol on the shelf. "Don't do it, Franz," he said quietly. "Just do as I say."

"But they will kill us," the mate protested through gritted teeth. "They are crazy."

"I don't think so, Franz. I think this man will keep his word. Stay calm."

Kleist returned his gaze to the shimmering windows, trying to peer out into the black night.

With Kleist manning the helm, Stauffen was free to look closely at the strange men around him. He knew they were supposed to be Romans.

He had studied European history in high school. They were dressed in filthy red tunics and heavily tarnished armor. The one called Lucius was older than the rest. His nearly black hair was long and unkempt. He never stopped looking out the windows at the east bank.

Fifteen minutes later, Stauffen saw the blinking red light of a buoy marking the far edge of the northbound lane. Past that was the gray line of the riverbank. "That is the spot. It is shallow there, but we can probably make it."

Lucius peered out the windows. "Yes. That will do."

Then a surge of water from upstream caught the towboat broadside, making it rock. "Hang on!" Stauffen shouted. "The water is rising with the rain."

A few minutes later, the shoreline was clearly visible in the deck lights. The east bank sloped steeply up into reeds and brush. Stauffen picked up the handset and spoke. "Lookouts, be ready. We may hit a sandbar. Call out if you see any rocks."

A tinny voice came from the speaker. "Aye, sir. The riverbank is all mud and sand. The barge is about twenty meters from the water's edge."

"Very well. Hold on." He glanced at the digital depth gauge and turned to Kleist. "Eight meters. Ease off. There will be surges as we get closer. Give her some port rudder to keep us in deeper water."

The barge, for all its size and weight, only drew about half a meter of water. The towboat's keel was four meters below the waterline.

Suddenly, *Rhein Königin* rolled violently. Plutonius slipped on the slick deck and fell, dropping his gladius. In a flash, Kleist let go of the wheel and grabbed for the gun under the console.

"Franz! No!" Stauffen shouted.

Kleist yanked the pistol from its holster and pointed it at Lucius's head.

Marcus recognized what the man was holding and lunged at him, grabbing his wrist. Kleist twisted out of his grasp and swung the heavy pistol across Marcus's face. Then he aimed it toward Lucius and pulled the trigger. A bright yellow flash and earsplitting blast erupted in the small wheelhouse. Lucius was blinded by the flash. Crassius slammed backward against the rear wall. He slid to the deck with a bright red flower of blood appearing on his shoulder. Kleist hit the button for the on-deck bullhorn. "I have their commander! Come to the wheelhouse now!"

Stauffen's eyes widened in shock. "Franz! Look out!" He saw the big man coming up behind his first mate. There was a flash of gleaming steel.

Kleist whirled, trying to point the Beretta at his attacker, but Marcus viciously shoved the entire length of his gladius into the mate's belly.

Plutonius, who had gotten to his feet, clumsily bashed his sword's pommel against Stauffen's head. The towboat captain reeled from the blow but held the back of the helmsman's chair and stayed on his feet. "Franz, you damned fool . . ."

The two men who'd been on the bow ran into the wheelhouse. Plutonius and Sestus lunged at them. August ran away only to be stabbed by a legionary from behind. He fell, shrieking in pain. Hans Schmidt shoved Lucius aside and tried to get at the radio. Again, Marcus stabbed and the man's eyes went blank, the radio handset still in his dying grip. It had all happened in one terrible minute.

With no hand at the helm, the boat rolled even more violently. A sharp lurch threw Stauffen to the deck, where he lay in the blood and rainwater. He managed to grab the wheel. Through the sickening pain in his head, he shot a look at the depth gauge. It read four meters. Not enough. He spun the wheel to port, trying to get the barge and boat out into deeper water and save something, anything at all. But he was too late. As they steadied themselves on the pitching deck, another violent lurch jolted the boat. The barge had run aground. Dozens of legionaries fell over or into the foaming water below. The *Rhein Königin's* bow crumpled like cardboard against the massive steel vessel. With a scream of fear, the cook struck his head on the throttles, crushing his forehead. He died almost instantly. Stauffen crashed into the armored glass of the wheelhouse and fell in a dazed heap. Lucius and the other Romans were saved from concussion by their helmets, but they grabbed at the console and chairs to remain on their feet.

Rhein Königin came to a sudden stop, the engines grinding to a halt when the propellers bit into the silt. For a long moment, the only sound was the rain beating on the roof and windows.

Plutonius bent to look at Crassius. "Sire, he is still alive. Can we take him with us?"

Lucius nodded. "We will not leave him behind."

Septimus ran into the wheelhouse. "Sire, are you injured? Many have fallen into the river." He stopped, seeing the blood-soaked deck. "I am too late, I see."

Lucius pointed at the barge. "Bring two men in here to carry Crassius to the bank. He is badly wounded, but we cannot help him now. Get the rest of the men to the bank and into cover. We must depart before someone comes." Septimus and the others moved off, leaving Lucius alone in the chaos of the wheelhouse.

He bent down to Stauffen. "Captain," he said, placing his hand on the other man's arm. "I am sorry. This was not my intention." Then he left the wheelhouse and saw the dead crewmen lying on the deck. Their blood was turning a pale pink in the rain. The wheelhouse doors were left open, and the rain sloughed across the bloody deck.

"Throw the dead men into the water," he said to Marcus.

The wet and seasick legionaries climbed down from the barge and dashed up the muddy riverbank. They waited in the dark brush as Lucius approached.

At last, Lucius reached solid ground. Behind him, the looming shape of the towboat and barge disappeared in the rain-rent darkness. Legio LIV Vindicta had finally reached Germania. The last part of their long journey was about to begin.

CHAPTER XVI

TRAIL OF BLOOD

Braden was back at work. He'd been able to catch six hours of sleep after the flight from Reims. By noon, he'd written a report on how his findings in France pertained to the Hodges case, watched a video deposition, researched a case involving the rape of a Belgian woman by a drunken American officer, and returned all his calls and emails. Just as he was considering going out for lunch, he heard a knock at his door, and Barney Rabble came in.

"Have a nice trip?" the other man asked as he sat down across from Braden.

"Yes, it was very interesting." He regarded Rabble with a jaundiced eye. "Don't you have your own office, Barn? Why do you always bug me at my desk?"

"You know how messy it is in there," Rabble said. "Besides, I like it in here. Quiet. Nothing ever happens in here."

"I wish," Braden said. "What's been happening while I was gone? Did World War Three start yet?" It was an old joke at NATO, especially since the Soviet Union's breakup in 1991. But as Jonathan Howard had put it, the world still had dragons.

"Not yet," Rabble said. "Got a minute?"

Braden shrugged. "I guess so. I was going to get some lunch, but I can wait. What do you have?"

"As if things in France and Belgium weren't weird enough, I just pulled this fax off the secure line. It's from the BKA."

"Germany," Braden said.

"Yeah, the Bundeskriminalampt is investigating a Rhine River towboat and barge found grounded on the bank north of Koblenz. All the crew are missing except for the captain, who was unconscious in the wheelhouse."

"When did this happen?"

"Last night. The towboat, named *Rhein Königin,* had anchored on the west bank twenty klicks north of Koblenz. A big storm knocked out their radar. They decided to tie up rather than risk moving in the dark during the storm. Apparently, they found a quiet spot on the west bank to anchor even though that was the southbound side of the river. They reported to their home office that they were staying put until daylight. The captain was a career sailor named . . ." He consulted the papers, "Heinrich Stauffen. Thirty years at sea in the Naval Auxiliary and on the river. A crew of five. They were due in Rotterdam at 1400 hours tomorrow. But when they failed to call in this morning, a call went out. No response. The river patrol boats were notified, and they found it right away. It was hard aground fifteen kilometers north of where it had anchored, near an abandoned sand and gravel mill."

"Did it just go adrift?" Braden asked.

"That's what they first thought. But the towboat's screws were half out of water and badly bent. That means they were moving under power. The barge was hard aground. Then, there's the blood."

"Blood? What blood?" Braden frowned and leaned forward.

"Didn't I mention that? Sorry." Rabble faked a sheepish smile. "Yes, there was blood all over the pilothouse and in the wardroom. The rain had washed some of it away, but there was still plenty of it."

"Damn you, Barn," Braden growled. "I don't need your games after I've had only a few hours' sleep. Where did the blood come from? The crew?"

"Evidently," Rabble said, unfazed. "A Beretta 9mm was lying on the pilothouse deck. It had been fired once. They found a bullet in the rear bulkhead. The investigators found blood on it, so it may have passed through a body before lodging in the wall. There is enough blood to be from several men. Large wounds."

"Where is the captain now?"

"Koblenz hospital under close supervision. He's got a bad concussion. He's a good man," Rabble said, anticipating Braden's next question. "He is respected by his crew and company. Not the type to go berserk and hack his men to death. He'll probably be able to tell what happened when he wakes up. They're dragging the river, looking for the crew. Something will turn up soon. I thought this might fit into our search for weird occurrences."

"I guess it does," Braden agreed, taking the report from Rabble. "Thanks a heap, Barn."

Rabble took a paper clip from Braden's desk. "Any luck on tracing those swords to the Roman cellar?"

"Nothing yet." He outlined what he'd learned and the plan to have weapons sent to Montrose to compare them with the wounds on St. Paul and Dumont. "I can't wait to hear the results." He read the fax.

Rabble was twisting the paper clip into a star. "Do you think the swords and the . . . what did you call them, the pilum, come from the cellar?"

"I hope they don't. It would really hurt the discovery since it means someone has tampered with the find, and nothing in it can be trusted as genuine."

The star looked more like a mutant jellyfish, but Rabble continued to twist. "That's too bad. What's your gut feeling?"

"Don't have one. We'll have to see. I might hear from Montrose today or tomorrow." Braden read down to the last page of the fax. His breath caught in his throat. "Damn."

Rabble looked up, a crooked smile on his face. The star was almost perfect.

"The barge and boat," Braden said, still reading. "They were found on the German side of the river."

Rabble nodded. "Yep. I noticed that. Seems strange, doesn't it?"

"The river's almost two klicks wide in some places. A boat adrift would end up on the west bank farther downstream."

"Yep," Rabble said again, still working on his star.

Braden shook his head. "This is giving me more weird vibes, Barn. Thanks for bringing this to me."

"Just doing my part for the cause. I gotta go." The paper clip, now twisted beyond all hope of ever holding together two pages, was tossed into the trash can. Rabble was reaching for the door when a knock sounded. He opened it, seeing one of the communications technicians standing there. "Hey, Katy, what's up?"

She smiled. "Hi, Barney. This just came in from the BKA. It's about that towboat, and I knew you were bringing it to Alex." She handed him the fax and walked away.

Braden heard the exchange. "More?"

Rabble closed the door and let his eyes roam down the page. "Yeah, you could say that. A man was found."

"Alive?"

Rabble shook his head. "His body was found in some wetlands near where the boat had first tied up."

"How was he killed?" Braden was almost sure he knew.

"Stabbed. Under the ribs. A deep, wide wound. His name was Klaus Steinmann. He was a deckhand on the *Rhein Königin*."

"Looks like the boat was hijacked, doesn't it?"

Rabble nodded. "Sure does. But who in the hell would hijack a towboat and a huge lumber barge in the middle of a storm to go fifteen klicks downriver to the other side? There are a dozen bridges within fifty klicks."

Someone who wants to get across the river without using a bridge, Braden thought.

"Well, you can add this to your other *Twilight Zone* stuff," Rabble said as he tossed the fax on Braden's desk and left the office.

A quick glance at the clock told Braden it was a good time to go to lunch. He picked up his coat and reached for the door when his phone rang.

"Drat, almost made it," he said, about to let his voicemail take it. But he threw the coat on his chair and grabbed the phone. "Alex Braden," he said.

"Ah, Mister Braden," said the accented voice. "This is Hugo Montrose from Bastogne. Have I caught you at a bad time?"

"Not at all, Doctor. I'm surprised to hear from you so soon. What can I do for you?"

"I received the weapons from Doctor Kelly yesterday and have been working with them all morning," Montrose said.

Braden walked around his desk and sat down. "Oh. Anything interesting?"

"You might say that. That charming Doctor Kelly sent me four swords, all superficially similar. She tagged them each with a letter, 'A' through 'D.' I was to find the one which made the wounds, but I would not know from what source each came."

Braden had a list of the specific swords and their sources on his desk. "Yes, Doctor. Please go on." He quickly read the list.

> **Sample A:** Reproduction Roman Gladius, Type Mainz-Fulham. Not authentic. New purchase.
>
> **Sample B:** Original weapon, Roman Gladius, Type Pompeii. Found 1951, Northern England, site 654451.00. Circa AD 42. Catalogue No. 11120.455. Collection of Cranfield University.
>
> **Sample C:** Original weapon, Roman Gladius, Type VI Harris-Germanicus. Found 2021, Robert Vineyards cellar, site 654511. Circa AD 14. Catalogue No.0014. No collection claim.
>
> **Sample D:** Reproduction Roman Gladius, Type Pompeii II. Not authentic. New purchase.

Montrose began. "We had done a computer modeling of the entry and cut wounds when we first examined the bodies. I was easily able to compare the different sword types to the size of the wound. And I have determined, without any doubt, the sword which killed Dumont was of a type included among the samples Doctor Kelly sent to me."

"Which one?" Braden held his breath, looking at the list again. One entry held his attention.

The Belgian medical examiner paused. "The first and fourth were slightly too narrow to be the correct one. And the second had too long a tapered point."

"I understand. So the one that was used in the killings was . . . ?"

"Sample C."

Braden felt a tiny chill in his chest. There it was.

Sample C: Original weapon, Roman Gladius, Type VI Harris-Germanicus. Found 2021, Robert Vineyards cellar.

"Damn." He didn't realize he'd spoken aloud.

"What was that?" Montrose's voice broke into his thoughts.

"I'm sorry. I was reading over the list of swords she gave me. I found the one you indicated."

"And what does it tell you?"

"The weapon was obtained from a Roman cellar just unearthed in France about a week ago. It was apparently looted prior to its discovery. It looks like several weapons were taken, and who knows what else."

"I see. Now, as to the spears. As we discussed yesterday afternoon, you told me it was probably a spear and not an arrow. With that information it was easier to understand the nature of the wounds. We had pieces of St. Paul's first lumbar vertebrae, which had been split by the weapon. It bore traces of black metal smears and embedded fragments. A metallurgical examination confirms that it was iron, not steel or bronze. The composition was crude, not modern at all. And the sample spear sent to us by Doctor Kelly was a perfect match. The metallurgical examination matched to within 99.7 percent. Seems we have a case of two stolen authentic Roman weapons used in these murders. At least four if you count the three different spears."

"I'm sure you're right." Braden had a thought. "By the way, did you find a match for that river silt in St. Paul's wound?"

"Yes, actually, we did."

"Was it from the Meuse River?"

There was a long silence. "How could you know that?" Montrose asked.

"Just a hunch," Braden replied. "I'm very grateful for your time and effort. Can you send me a copy of your report? I'll send you the list of the samples for your records. You've been very helpful. It looks like we have some artifact thieves and killers out there somewhere." Then he stopped, remembering the sailor. "Oh, and one more thing. A German towboat crewman was found murdered on the west bank of the Rhine this morning. He was killed with a large bladed weapon. You might want to contact whoever is conducting the autopsy. Your findings might be useful to them."

"I'll do that," Montrose said. "Thank you. If you need anything else, please don't hesitate to call. It is I who is in your debt."

Braden no longer felt like eating.

That evening he called Morley and gave him the news.

"I just knew you would be trouble when you arrived at our cellar," Morley chuckled. "Ah, well. I suppose we'll just have to be that much more precise in our research. We shall survive. I only hope they find the men responsible before any more people are killed."

Braden didn't have the heart to tell him about the towboat's missing crew and the dead sailor. There might not be a connection. Fat chance.

Two hours later, after heating up some leftovers and catching up on personal emails, he sat on the living room couch. He turned on the satellite TV and automatically went to the History Channel. He hoped he'd find something that would help him relax enough to go to sleep. The program was about the Bataan Death March. "Just what I need," he muttered. By the time the documentary of Allied prisoners of war who'd died on the march into Japanese captivity ended, Braden felt relaxed enough to consider going to bed. But sleep eluded him. It was after midnight when he finally drifted off into a troubled sleep.

He was walking down an endless dark stone corridor. There were closed doors on either side. Then the doors opened in quick succession, and thick clouds of white smoke poured out into the corridor. He stopped, unable to see. Then, thousands of men passed him. They wore red tunics and polished armor. There were no faces under the helmets, only dark and decayed skulls. Moldy shreds of dead flesh hung from their arms, legs, jaws, and empty eye sockets. They carried big swords and waved them over their heads, shouting in a language he didn't understand. They marched past, not paying him any attention. They climbed up a long stone stairway. Following them, he emerged into an icy cold night. The armored skeletons approached a dark and forbidding forest. The trees were like black bones shrouded in a thick mass of dark cobwebs like an immense deadly spider's web. The army of dead men marched in and disappeared from view. He tried to follow, but the web closed and cut off all entry into the forest. He looked down and saw his bare feet sinking into a pool of deep red mud. It was blood. Gallons and gallons of blood ran out from under the intertwined web hiding the forest. He was mired in a river of muddy gore. He could not run. But then he heard a voice calling out from the black forest. "Vindicta!"

Braden awoke with a start. He was in near-total darkness and for several seconds didn't know where he was. He was shaking, and his skin was covered in cold sweat. Then he heard the muted sound of a car passing by outside his bedroom window. A glance at the clock told him he'd been asleep for less than an hour. "What a fucking nightmare," he gasped. He knew it hadn't been real, but he glanced at his feet poking out from the twisted covers to be sure they didn't have bloody mud on them. "No more sleep for you, pal," he grumbled. He went into the bathroom and relieved himself, trying to think of what he could do to rid himself of the nightmarish visions. A beer sounded good, so he took one from the refrigerator. Twisting off the bottle cap, he took a long pull, tasting the strong brew on his tongue and throat. He expelled a long breath. A minute later the bottle was empty. Then he pulled the cap from another beer and went into the living room, passing by the half-open window overlooking the street. The night was almost dead quiet. He took another drink of the beer and sighed. For a moment he thought of calling Ann, but dismissed it. No sense in screwing up her sleep. Might as well watch some more TV. But he'd sworn off History Channel for the night.

He checked the satellite TV listings and found a panel discussion of the German situation. That should be nice and boring. "Channel 54," he said aloud and hit the buttons on the remote. The picture changed to a group of men and women dressed in suits seated around a curved table.

Speaking in German with English and French subtitles, the panel talked about Germany's possible withdrawal from NATO. Braden watched as he finished the second beer, but he could not focus on the discussion. Something had clicked in his mind. What was it?

He tried to recall his exact motions of a few minutes before and saw the remote in his lap. He picked it up. Clicking on "Info" he saw the channel appear on the screen. "Fifty-four," he said again. He racked his beer-buzzed brain. Fifty-four equals vengeance. He wiped his face with his hand.

"Shit, I'm turning into a basket case." Sleep. That was what he needed. Lots of sleep. "Should get some of that plant. That would knock me out fast enough," he chuckled. Lots of sleep. Then as if he'd been hit with an electric shock, his eyes snapped open. "No, it can't be. Oh my God!"

He snatched up his cell phone. Checking his contact list, he selected the number. The electronic ringing tone came through the earpiece. A sleepy female voice came on. "Hello?"

"Sharon? It's Alex Braden. I'm sorry to be calling so late, but I have to speak to you. It's urgent. Really. Can we talk?"

"Can't it wait? It's past two in the morning."

"I'm sorry, but it can't wait."

Sharon sighed wearily. "Okay, just a moment." He heard the phone put down and some mumbling and shuffling. "I'm here. What is it?"

"I had to ask you something very important."

"I'm not fully awake yet, but I'm listening."

"I need to know what would happen if a large group of men, whose average age is about twenty-five, are in excellent physical condition in a tightly sealed environment with an ambient air temperature of five degrees Celsius, and were to fill the air with a high concentration of smoke from the Mallorcus plant. There is no one to monitor them or cleanse the air."

"Oh, for Christ's sake," Sharon sighed. "I told you. They'd eventually die."

"How long could they live?"

"What are you driving at?"

"I have a crazy thought, but I need verification. How long?"

"How long do you want? A decade? Two? Ten?"

"As long as possible. Just go way beyond rational thought and logic, Sharon." He held his breath.

"Fine," she grumbled. "I don't know all of the particular properties of the plant, but under the conditions you propose, I guess they could live for several decades. But that's just not realistic."

He took the plunge. "Could they live for two thousand years?"

Sharon snorted. "Are you out of your mind?"

"I hope not," he said seriously.

She laughed mirthlessly. "I'll tell you this. The plant does have incredible preservative properties. It slows metabolism to almost nothing. With a near-freezing air temperature, the body would slow down even more. So it might be possible that a person would simply be clinically dead, the brain stops and the body totally inert. No consumption of energy." Sharon expelled a breath. "It's a helluva long reach, Alex. Two thousand damn years. I was willing to concede a couple of decades. But you're past that by a factor of one hundred. Think about it."

"Believe me, Sharon. I have. And I'm dead certain I'm right. The men in that cellar went in there for one purpose. To put themselves to sleep for a long time."

"For two thousand years? Give me a break."

"I don't know why they did it, but that's the only thing that explains the bodies in those collapsed rooms. The ones in such perfect condition. How else can that be logically explained? The rest were little more than skeletons. How can there be such a difference in the same place?"

"They might have been interred years later," Sharon pointed out, but her voice betrayed uncertainty.

"Even if they'd been put in there five hundred years later, they'd still be little more than bone. I think the men in those rooms were still alive in hibernation when the ceiling fell in and crushed them." He frowned, trying to remember something. An important detail.

"Simmer down," Sharon said. "We're having autopsies performed to see how and when they died. I'm still not convinced."

Braden racked his sleep-deprived brain. An image of the cellar's long central hallway played across his mind's eye. On each side were doors.

The doors! That was what he'd been trying to remember. "The doors into the rooms. There was some sort of leather trim on them. It reminded me of a gasket or weather seal."

"Yes," Sharon said. "We found it curious that the rooms which had no bodies or had suffered collapse had intact doors and seals. Probably a coincidence."

"No. Those doors were meant to seal in the smoke. In the rooms where the smoke dissipated, the men died ages ago. Otherwise, they lived for much longer." Braden was on a roll. "You said it yourself. The Romans knew more about herbs and natural medicine than we know today. They found a way to extend life in hibernation. And it worked until the fumes leaked out. Then they awoke and emerged."

"But how in the hell could you even think such a thing?" Sharon persisted. "This is totally impossible."

Braden told Sharon about the strange sightings and incidents across France and Belgium. "People have seen men wearing Roman armor. Men killed with Roman weapons. Missing livestock." He paused. "Hang on a second, Sharon." He walked over to the couch and opened his shoulder bag. Inside he found the map he and Rabble had used and unrolled it on the dining room table. "This morning, a Rhine River towboat turned up with a dead and missing crew." He picked up a pencil and put a mark on the bank of the Rhine River north of Koblenz. Using the straight edge of a folder, he placed one end on the towboat's location and the other on the cellar. "Ho-lee shit," he hissed.

"Now what?" Sharon asked over the phone.

He stared at the map. The folder edge followed the dots of each report right from the French teens, the railroad sighting, the murdered policemen, and the missing livestock. There was a clear line stabbing out of France, across Belgium, and straight into Germany. *I wasn't wrong. It's really happening.* He took a breath and said it aloud for the first time. "Sharon, I believe a living Roman Legion is on the march to the east."

Sharon let out a surprised laugh. "A Roman Legion from the first century? Are you totally insane? Or is this the plot for a Sci-Fi movie?"

"Don't you see? Nothing in this affair makes any sense at all, and the only workable solution is impossible."

"A living Roman Legion." There was no mistaking the skepticism in her voice.

"Yes. If you just forget that it's impossible, then every single thing fits together perfectly. And that's what I think is happening."

Sharon let out a long sigh. "I guess you're right. But it's still not possible." Braden heard less conviction in her voice. But she continued. "Anyway, I left out one thing."

He rubbed his eyes. "What's that?"

"The mortality factor. It's theoretically possible for a large group of healthy men to live for years in a coma, or hibernation, if you will, but I can't see more than a few of them living so long."

"How many?"

"Impossible to say for sure, but if you forced me to give you a number, I'd say no more than one in five, perhaps one in four might survive."

Braden sighed. "That's what I wanted to hear. Thank you, Sharon."

"What? What'd I say?"

"The cellar was built to hold forty-eight hundred men. There are more than thirty-six hundred bodies or remains. Nearly twelve hundred are unaccounted for. One in four, Sharon."

"Shit." It was obvious she'd thought her final argument would convince him. "Okay, fine. But you have no proof."

"I think I do. The DNA of the seven blood samples from the murder scene was run through the world DNA ID database. Two were the cops, but the other five were totally unidentified."

Sharon's voice showed real surprise. "Really? But that's supposed to be impossible."

"Tell me about it," he said with a chuckle. "But there's more. They did a generation check on the DNA to find any living relatives to see if they could ID the blood that way. The database found about ninety people whose DNA was descended from the same family line as three of the samples. All were from Mediterranean stock. But the real shocker was the number of generations they were descended."

"How many?"

"About seventy-five to eighty generations. Two thousand years. Now it makes perfect sense."

"Wow. Well, I think you'll have a rough time convincing anyone, Alex," she said kindly. "I'll help you if I can."

"I'm grateful," he said and meant it.

"Do you intend to call Arthur?"

"Later on, I do. I need to solidify my thoughts first."

She laughed. "But me you'll call in the middle of the night. I feel so honored. If you're right, then tell me this. What are these Romans up to? Where are they going?"

"That's a good question. I don't know. Rome, maybe."

She laughed again. "Oh, I can see it now. CNN will eat that up."

Braden wasn't listening. He was still looking at the map with the folder on it. On the face of the folder was a note he'd written of a trial date for a soldier charged with drug possession. November 17-19, 2021. His eyes narrowed in thought. He slid the folder aside but then put it back in place, looking at the imaginary line he'd created. It ended at the Rhine, but there had to be more. Where were the Romans going? What was their plan? A fleeting thought passed through his mind like a silent train. Seventeenth to the nineteenth. Seventeen. Eighteen. Nineteen. He quickly jotted the numbers down in a column. The sum jumped out at him, and a tingling buzz went through his entire body. "God, it really fits. Goddamn!"

Sharon's voice cut into his thoughts. "What was that, Alex?"

"Sharon, what do seventeen, eighteen, and nineteen add up to?"

"Oh, for crying out loud," she muttered in exasperation. "Give me a break, will you?"

"Please, Sharon," he persisted. "What do they add up to?"

"Uh, fifty . . . fifty-four. Why?"

"What does that number mean to you?"

"Look, I'm tired and cranky. Give me a break, okay?"

"Fifty-four is the number of the legion in the cellar," Braden reminded her.

"Right. So what?"

"We know there were only thirty legions in the entire history of the Roman Army. That was one of the biggest mysteries in the cellar."

"But what does adding seventeen, eighteen, and nineteen have to do with anything, for God's sake?"

"Do you recall the Battle of the Teutoberg Forest?"

She sighed. "Of course I do. In AD 9. Varus and the three legions were massacred by the Germans. Nearly all were killed."

"Less than three hundred lived to escape," Braden said.

"Okay. But what—"

He cut her off. "The three legions destroyed in the Varian Disaster were the seventeenth, eighteenth, and nineteenth legions. After the massacre they were never again reformed." He paused. "Until the legion in the cellar. The fifty-fourth legion."

There was no reply from Sharon, but he heard her breathing.

"And there's more."

"What more could there be?" Her voice had a quaver to it.

"The name of the legion. It was 'VDCTA.' Arthur showed me a list of possible meanings for the letters."

"Go on," she said.

Braden said, "It means 'Vindicta.' Vengeance. Revenge. Punishment." He listened, but all he heard was the sound of breathing. "Sharon?"

Her voice was a mere ghost of sound. "Oh my God."

Coming soon:

The next story in the Vengeance of the Last Roman
Legion series: *Legionary*.

ACKNOWLEDGMENTS

This book has undergone scores of rewrites and edits over a period of ten years. It bears little resemblance to the original version, which ran to about 150,000 words. Now it is a four-part series totaling more than a quarter of a million words. It still amazes me that I wrote this book. But I did not do it myself. Yes, I did the writing, the research, and the endless rewrites, but I was only the spearpoint of a large team of wonderful people who aided, encouraged, and even drove me to keep going and finish the damn book.

Authors of written works rarely take full credit for their accomplishments, at least the honest ones. I am glad and honored to acknowledge the contributions of so many people. A bit of background will help. I am blind and have been so for nearly twenty years, long before I began this book. But I was already a historian, writer, and aspiring bestselling author, the latter still in the future. I work and write with a complex array of technology and tools that make it possible for me to live and work with confidence.

But thanks to these tools, I was only faced with the same challenges that any sighted writer deals with—that of coming up with a story and putting it on paper. That was the hard part, not being blind. In any event, being a blind writer has few serious obstacles other than those we all face in the ever-changing world of computers and software. I am extremely grateful to my longtime friend Don Ramm, a former Air Force pilot, who, for some reason that still baffles me, has spent hundreds of hours to keep my computers and hardware working. I depend on my internet connections, email, and network to do my job. If Don had not been there for me, I'd have to write my books like Fred Flintstone, with a slate and chisel, or with Windows Vista, which would be even worse. My email would be smoke signals and my phone a pair of tin cans and a string. Don, you are a true and devoted friend. I could never earn enough in royalties to repay you for all your work. I am truly grateful. May the wind always be under your wings.

I am glad to offer my gratitude to my good friend Linda Stull, who gave so much of her time and effort to seeing my dreams come true. Every book and nearly every article I have written went under her careful, patient, and precise scrutiny. She read every word, and even though we often disagreed on certain points, we now agree that this is a far better book as a result.

My parents Eric and Margit Carlson gave me a love of history and reading but did not live to see my first book published. But I think of them with every book I write, hoping they know that I am carrying on the legacy they left me. My cousin, Katerina Petersson, was a fan of my writing and encouraged me to keep it up. Like my mother, she instilled a love of reading and history that opened the world of the past to my hungry mind and imagination.

My older brother David and I shared a love of history and reading, and he was an excellent sounding board for ideas and suggestions.

My buddy Rob Wood and his sweet wife, Elaine, spent a great deal of time helping me move forward after Jane's death. I can never express enough gratitude to them for all they have done. My friends John and Anita Campbell, neighbors Carol Gendel, Kate Rogelstad Janelle Personius, John and Geneva Tolbert, John and Mary Lou Rushing, Gigi Harrington, Kimmy Aguinaldo, and other residents of Madrid Manor were the Earthbound angels in my life.

My brothers and sisters at Hope United Methodist Church, like the warm and caring people they are, gave so much to help me move forward and not give up. John and Linda Missoni, Vince and Lynn Cramer, Pastor Brian Kent, Paul Swaykowski, and the members of the Thursday Knights Bible Study group were always there when I needed them. I have never known such comfort and contentment from any group of people in my life. May God bless them all.

Back when I was first considering this book, I became involved with a Roman Legion reenactment group in San Diego. Legio IX Hispaña was run by a colorful and only slightly mad Irishman named Sean Richards. I learned a lot about the life of a Roman legionary from the men of Legio IX. My closest friend in the legion was Optio Mario Padillo. Tall, strong, and handsome with dark wavy hair and chiseled features, Mario looks like Central Casting's idea of a Roman centurion. He helped me understand what it was like for the legionaries of the first century. From the start he was enthusiastic about this book project, even going so far as to urge me to get it published in 2009, the two thousandth anniversary of the Varian Disaster. But since I had not yet even started the manuscript, and this was in 2008, that was unlikely.

For three years I was a member of the prestigious Rancho Bernardo Writers' Group, headed by Peter Berkos, an avuncular and supportive leader. He and the other members of the RBWG read my manuscript and provided excellent (although not always heeded) advice. They helped make this book far better than it was. Maryjane Roe, Mo Kindle, Terry Ambrose, Manjula Panday, and the others are all writers and authors. I very much hope to see their books alongside mine in bookstores.

My relationships with the Pearl Harbor Survivors Association, Distinguished Flying Cross Society, Order of Daedelians, American Ex-POWs, Commemorative Air Force, San Diego Air & Space Museum, and many other organizations have enriched my life and provided a wealth of articles, interviews, and friendships. I am proud to be friends with many members of the Navy, Army, Marine Corps, other veterans, and NASA astronauts. More than a few were World War II, Korean War, and Vietnam War veterans. While none had any direct connection with the armies of the Roman Empire, they often provided a keen insight into the mind of the soldier. For these people, who have been my biggest fans and supporters, I give my everlasting gratitude.

For the greater glory of Rome!

Mark Carlson
Augustus MMXXII

ABOUT THE AUTHOR

MARK CARLSON, a resident of San Diego has been a lifelong student of military history. Legally blind, he works with advanced software on his computer and travels with a Guide Dog. He has never considered his blindness to be an obstacle, only a challenge.

For the past twenty years Carlson has been a regular contributor to more than a dozen military history publications. In that time, he has written over two hundred articles and interviewed hundreds of veterans, actors, historians and authors. A former Civil War and Roman re-enactor, Carlson has gained an insight into the world of the fighting man to bring depth and realism into his writing. He is very passionate about history, considering it an obligation to remember the past with respect.

His last book, published by Sunbury Press, *The Marines Lost Squadron: The Odyssey of VMF-422*, was highly acclaimed by respected military historians.

His magazine articles run the gamut of topics from aviation, naval, and military history, classic film and television, dogs, humor, and essays. He started by writing stories about his first Guide Dog, Musket, and later, about his work at the San Diego Air & Space Museum.

A former president of a San Diego Toastmasters club, he tours the country doing lectures on history for colleges and adult education programs. A popular speaker for several national military museums and groups, he is a member of several veteran and historical organizations.

Out of the Darkness is his first novel.

Made in the USA
Middletown, DE
06 April 2022

63696982R00118